Diamondvale: Shattered Memories

Eric Hua

Published by Eric Hua, 2024.

DIAMONDVALE: SHATTERED MEMORIES

First edition. March 22, 2024.

Copyright © 2024 Eric Hua.

ISBN: 978-1738040742

Written by Eric Hua.

Table of Contents

This book is written for my grade 6 class of 2023/2024.

Thank you to Netanya who designed the title page for this book!

Thank you to Aria who designed the picture on the back cover!

Diamondvale: Shattered Memories

Zenith / Nadir

Here lies the prosperous city of Zenith, a place powered and maintained by crystals known as Geode-stones. It has a lively marketplace where most civilians gathered to go about their business. Despite having the majority of the population within the area, the most significant place within Zenith would be the massive school in the heart of the city known as Diamondvale.

Zenith was a place where education and progress were valued above all things. Inside Diamondvale was where the great prodigal minds and warriors honed their skills to continually advance their city. Within the walls of the school was a student in his early 20s, inside a secluded room, training for a major event.

He was deep in meditation until his focus was broken by the sound of the opening door. A rush of anger came before him, and he was ready to unleash a mouthful on the person who disrupted his training until he saw who it was.

"Arnav! Why am I not surprised to find you here?"

"Headmaster Volice!" He bowed in respect.

"Formalities are overrated! Rise, and I do apologize for disturbing your meditation."

"No need to apologize, but to what do I owe the honour? I'm sure someone of your calibre has more important things to do than to visit a student."

"Do not be so modest, my boy. In a few days, you have the chance to advance into the elite class within Diamondvale."

"Thank you for the kind words, Headmaster, but others before me have completed such a task. I don't see why mine should deserve more attention."

"Arnav, I hate to say it, but the quality of students at Diamondvale isn't what it used to be. It's been a long time since someone has even come close to reaching the Diamond-ranked Class. Your examination isn't just about your advancement, it's also about giving hope to the other students that they can one day accomplish what you have done."

"I had no idea. Forgive me Headmaster Voice."

"No need to apologize. Sound familiar?"

"Haha, you got me with that one."

"I will leave you be. Good luck with your examination tomorrow."

"I will do my best!"

As Voice left the room and shut the door behind him, Arnav returned to his meditation. The headmaster then turned away and began heading down the halls of the school.

Further down were two of the school's police enforcers. One was an experienced ranked officer while the other seemed new to the job.

"LISTEN UP PRIVATE! DO YOU HAVE ANY IDEA HOW IMPORTANT YOUR CURRENT JOB IS?"

"Uh, no sir, not really." The private sounded confused.

"THAT IS NOT GOOD ENOUGH PRIVATE! WE HAVE A SWORN DUTY TO KEEP THE STUDENTS AND ALL THE ARCHIVES OF DIAMONDVALE SAFE FROM ALL INTRUDERS!"

"Okay."

"WHAT KIND OF RESPONSE IS THAT? DO YOU KNOW WHAT WOULD HAPPEN IF HEADMASTER VOICE HEARD YOUR ATTITUDE?"

"Ummm." He tried to get the enforcer to look behind him but he continued rambling.

"HEADMASTER VOLICE WOULD EAT YOU UP FOR BREAKFAST IF HE HEARD THAT ATTITUDE OF YOURS! I HOPE HE ISN'T AROUND TO SEE THIS RIGHT NOW BECAUSE..."

The loud enforcer heard someone clearing their throat behind him. He felt his heart sink and he was beginning to sweat as he slowly turned around to meet the person behind him.

"HEADMASTER VOLICE! I WAS JUST TALKING ABOUT YOU AND UH..." The Headmaster ignored his comment and made his way to the much younger enforcer.

"Tell me, young enforcer, what is your name?" His voice was calm yet it demanded respect.

"It's Max."

"A great name. I don't know what you have been told but I only have one question to ask of you. Will you protect Diamondvale to the best of your abilities?"

"Yes." Max gave a stern reply as Volice looked him directly in the eyes with serious intent.

"Okay!" Suddenly, the serious look on the headmaster's face broke into a smile which threw Max off-guard. "I trust you will do a fine job." Added the Headmaster.

He then walked away leaving the rookie enforcer pondering about the interaction they just had. However, Max wouldn't have much time to assess as his loud supervisor told him to snap out of his daydreaming and get back to his post.

B elow the radiant city of Zenith, was the undercity known as Nadir. This city receives the toxic residues produced from the upper city. Chemical waste can be found dripping out of the sewage pipes throughout the city. Not to mention the dense fumes in the air that could affect one's mind. It was clear as night and day, that the people in Nadir did not enjoy the same luxury as the citizens of Zenith.

However, the people of Nadir were not be looked down upon. Forced to live under such harsh conditions, Nadir is home to some of the world's toughest fighters. Training inside a rundown gym was such a character.

Her hands were unarmed and she wore under armour beneath her training shirt and sweat pants, with an 'M' inked on her back shoulder. Standing on the opposite side of the ring was a training robot set to the highest difficulty: insanity. The robot began to show a countdown: 3, 2, 1! Then its eyes turned red and activated, signalling the battle simulation had begun.

The girl attempted to strike the robot first with a right jab but the robot analyzed the situation and perfectly countered by sliding then delivering a right hook to her stomach. She was taken aback and the robot did not let up, as it continued with a fury of jabs directed at the girl's face.

Thankfully the girl was well trained, as she held her arms up and managed to block the incoming assault. However, the robot read her blocks and changed up its attack pattern by kneeing her gut. The attack had her winded temporarily but little did the android know, that was exactly what the girl needed to wake her up.

Suddenly the look in her eyes shifted to one of seriousness and intense focus. The robot attacked with agility, striking from the right but the girl hopped back and then dashed forward to kick one of its target areas, awarding her some points.

Despite being pushed back, the robot re-engaged the battle but the fight had swung in the girl's favour. Her unorthodox fighting style which was a mix between dancing and martial arts, was too much for the training droid to handle. The fighter was untouchable with her fancy footwork, effortlessly kicking the robot at all the critical points.

Eventually, the time limit of the battle expired and the robot ceased its assault. With the battle over, the screen showed a new high score had been achieved, the person's name was Myla. The screen then loaded the next four highest scores, all under her name.

After finishing her training and cleaning up, Myla went to a local convenience store. There wasn't a huge selection of goods but Myla picked up a few bottles of water and soda before throwing some coins on the counter for the store owner, but before she could leave he called her out.

"Hey! You are short a couple of copper coins!"

"What? The price for this is two silver coins and one copper coin. It has never changed since I started coming here."

"Sorry missy, there's something called inflation."

"Tch."

"Hehe, now pay up!"

As Myla was about to fork over the extra copper coins, the store owner saw two girls leaving the store conspicuously. He ran out of his station and intercepted them at the exit.

"And just where do you two think you are going?"

"We are just leaving now sir. We didn't see anything from your store that we wanted." One of them replied.

"Is that so? Then what do you call this?!" He pulled some unpaid chocolate bars out of their pockets."

"What? How did that end up there? Must have slipped into our pockets or something." Replied the same girl.

"You can't fool me! You two are thieves! I shall have you reported to the officers at once!"

"Oh no this is bad. We're doomed!" cried the other girl.

Myla saw everything that transpired before her eyes. She knew the value of hard work and that actions have consequences but something about the girls made her have a slight change of heart. She threw more money at the feet of the shopkeeper.

"Will that suffice?"

"Ooooh, splendid! This should cover their cost plus yours! Thank you for your business!"

After the sleazy store clerk received his money, he left the girls alone. Myla was about to speak with them but one of the girls spoke up first.

"Sorry lady, we have a strict 'stranger danger policy' so we ain't talking to you! Come on Sissi, let's get out of here!" The first girl walked out the door leaving the one girl behind.

"Amrita, that's not very nice!" She was about to leave as well but she stopped for a moment. "Thank you for buying the chocolate for us, kind stranger lady!"

Myla was about to ask the girl to wait up but she felt a sudden pain in her head. The experience didn't last long but it was enough that Myla lost sight of the girls. Thinking her head pain was a result of overtraining, she headed home to rest.

Home for Myla was not the typical house most would be accustomed to. Instead, she lived in an inn owned by the innkeeper known as Sahil. When she entered the door, she immediately threw him the money to pay for her rent.

Sahil was shocked because normally he would have to pester her for the money. He was about to give her one of his witty remarks but Myla was not having it on this night. She told the innkeeper she was not in the mood to speak and went directly to her room and fell asleep.

ERIC HUA

Security Breach / The Unknown

Night had fallen on the skies of Zenith. It was difficult to believe that this radiant place during the day could seem so different in the dark. The streets were empty without a person in sight. Even Diamondvale had its facilities closed as the students that lived in the dorm all had a curfew to abide by. The only ones found in the halls in the night hours were the police enforcers. Most nights would be a quiet and boring for the enforcers but something was about to happen that no one in Diamondvale could anticipate.

A mysterious figure with his face concealed, hid on the rooftops of the school, surveying the movements of the officers as they patrolled the grounds. Once he had their walk cycles figured out, he began to make his way to his targeted destination.

All the guards were oblivious to the intruder's movements as he used the shadows and the walls to his advantage. In about seven minutes, he bypassed all the officers and managed to enter inside undetected.

He was now standing in front of a vault that required a passcode to enter. Confidently, he raised his hand and used his finger to enter the four-digit code. In only one attempt, the pad lit up without making a sound. The vault had been unlocked and the intruder walked in.

The room in which he entered was the archives of Diamondvale where they kept all their current and historical documents. There were numerous shelves all filled with books, scrolls, and other forms of records. With the vast knowledge accumulated in the room, the world could be doomed if it were to fall into the wrong hands. Knowing he had a limited amount of time, the thief began his search.

Outside of the vault, an experienced security guard passed by the keypad terminal and noticed an anomaly. He immediately called for backup but proceeded with caution into the archives.

After minutes of scouring through the shelves, the intruder had completed his mission. He was ready to leave when the campus guard attempted to sneak up on him with a crystal-powered stun baton. The intruder easily side-stepped the attack and then grabbed the guard by the collar and threw him against one of the shelves, knocking him unconscious.

The intruder tried to leave but again he was stopped, this time by an electric discharge that barely missed his neck. He turned around to see that reinforcements had arrived. There were five more security officers armed with crystal-powered staffs that were capable of releasing electrical shocks that could paralyze their targets.

The leader of the group ordered his team to arrest the intruder and together they attacked simultaneously. As they got closer to the enemy, the mysterious fighter threw down some crystals that exploded and created a blanket of smoke in the room. All the guards were now separated, unable to see one another, and were coughing because of the fumes. When the smoke cleared, the intruder was the only one left standing with all the guards defeated.

He thought he was clear to leave but there was one last guard that just appeared, it was Max. Despite seeing all his comrades defeated, he was not deterred by his enemy. Max rushed in with the crystal-charged baton in his hand and what should have been a routine dodge for the enemy didn't happen. Instead, as Max got closer with the crystal shining against his face, the mysterious man froze and took a hit.

Max had somehow gotten the upper hand and he was ready to hit the man once more to make sure he was immobilized but as the crystal baton got closer to the injured enemy, Max saw a symbol on the cloth armour. The man had the letter 'D' on his chest and upon seeing it, Max froze for a brief period. The intruder took that opportunity to throw a crystal that exploded into a smoke screen.

Shortly after the smoke cleared, the enemy had escaped. Max was about to chase after the intruder but he stopped as he felt his foot step on something. He looked down and picked up what looked to be an arrow. His mind began to drift off as he looked deeply at the arrow but he snapped back to reality when he heard reinforcements approaching the scene.

He guided them to where their injured comrades were and assisted them. However, things would never be the same for Max after that evening. He couldn't shake the feeling that he had seen the symbol on the intruder's armour before.

———— ✶⸢⸣⸤⸥ ————

B eyond the undercity of Nadir was the dangerous lands known as the 'Polluted Wilds.' It was well known that people who traverse the grounds during the night seldom return to the city. Many have gone missing and there have been no clues left behind. It was so dangerous that Nadir assigned a guard at the exit of the city to ensure no one left the premises during the night.

However, two mischievous girls managed to sneak by the guard post undetected and were free to roam the 'Polluted Wilds' on their own.

"Wow, I can't believe how easy it was to get past the outpost. They normally have someone there. Oh well, that's just our good luck right Sissi?" She didn't hear a response at first so she asked again. "Uh, Sissi?"

"Amrita, I'm getting a bad vibe from this place and it's making me sad. Maybe we shouldn't have come here."

"Sissi, where is your sense of wonder and adventure?" As she asked with enthusiasm, a creepy noise echoed through the area.

Amrita jumped as she was startled while Sissi somehow kept a straight face and with a gloomy tone she said, "We are doomed..."

After the noise subsided for a moment, Amrita regained her composure and tried to shrug it off as if nothing happened but then they heard a creepy wail. Both girls turned their attention to where they heard the sound and they were not prepared for what they had witnessed.

The archives inside Diamondvale had been closed off for investigation after an intruder trespassed on school grounds. Students gathered outside in the surrounding area, hoping to obtain more information. With so many uneasy thoughts amongst the students, murmurs and rumours began to spread.

Arriving late onto the scene was Arnav, who was at the very back of the crowd. He attempted to make his way to the front but the wall of people made it difficult to squeeze by. He was going to give it another try but as he was about to, someone called out for his attention.

It was a student named Ajay from a different class. Unlike Arnav who was an Emerald class (2nd highest) Ajay was a Sapphire (3rd highest).

"Slept in again didn't you?" Ajay asked.

"Hey, you're not the one who has a big examination coming up!"

"Haha relax Arnav, I'm only messing with you."

"So what's going on? Why is everyone gathered here? Is someone hurt?" Arnav had a million questions for Ajay who wasn't sure either but another voice came in.

"Oh come on, how can you two not know what's going on?" It was a girl named Netanya who was in the Ruby class.

"Whoa, I don't want to hear that coming from you, Netanya. You are in the lowest rank out of all of us!"

"Hey! If it weren't for my allergies I would be a higher rank than you!"

They were about to break into a heated argument but Arnav interrupted them. "Ajay now is not the time." He then turned to Netanya and asked nicely for a summary of what she knew.

She heard that an intruder managed to infiltrate the school and somehow sneak into the archives. When the school security caught wind of his presence, they attempted to stop him but they were all defeated.

"Is anyone...?" Arnav was afraid to ask.

"Oh everyone was reported to sustain no major injuries and most of them will make a speedy recovery within the day!"

"That's a relief," Arnav replied.

"I'm sure there is nothing to worry about. The enforcers will figure this out in no time and have that intruder arrested!" Ajay announced confidently.

"You three are clueless aren't you?" Another voice appeared and it was one that was well-distinguished and known by nearly everyone in the school. It was from the student in the Diamond class and arguably the highest-ranked student in the school, Harshitha.

Ajay and Netanya were too stunned by her presence to speak but Arnav was not. "What do you mean?"

"Sigh, do you even know how the Diamondvale defence system works?" Harshitha questioned.

"Yeah of course I do!" Ajay sounded confident but then he whispered over to Netanya. "Psh, how does the defence system work?"

Netanya pushed her glass up and then went into lecture mode. "The defence system in Diamondvale is powered by the Geode-stones throughout the entire campus. It has a special defence recognition system that will only respond against people who aren't residents of the school!"

"Wow, not bad for a Ruby-ranked. I would give you a 'B' for your answer." Harshitha responded.

"What?! Only a 'B'?! What more could I have said to get an 'A'?!" Netanya was flabbergasted as she couldn't figure it out but Arnav finally got the hint of what Harshitha was getting at.

"Yesterday night, none of the alarms sounded..."

"Wait, you mean to say that the intruder is, SOMEONE FROM THE SCHOOL?!?" Netanya finished Arnav's thought.

"What are we going to do? Are we in danger? Is Arnav's examination going to get cancelled tomorrow?" Ajay blurted out questions in panic.

Before anything else could be said, an announcement was made to everyone. It called for the students to resume their schedule as normal as the investigation continued.

Many of the students were disappointed, as they were hoping that classes would be cancelled for the day. But the bigger concern was the element of uncertainty that was now within the back of everyone's mind. How safe was Diamondvale after its security was easily breached and was the intruder among them?

Ajay and Netanya had already left for their classes with Arnav about to go but Harshitha had some final words for him. "It appears your examination will continue as scheduled tomorrow. I bid you good luck to whichever of my classmates you face."

He wasn't sure if she meant what she said. Thinking she was done, he was about to head to his class but she had more to add. "Also, be careful who you put your trust in." She left with those words which left Arnav even more confused.

The Request

After the investigation was completed, the captain of the enforcers, wearing an 'S' emblem on his shoulder, made his way over to the Headmaster's office to deliver the news. He presented the information they uncovered and everything they knew about the situation.

"That is all you have to report?"

"Yes, Headmaster Volice. The intruder was extremely cunning and did not leave behind any clues. Therefore, there are no possible suspects so far."

"And what of the archives? What did he take?"

"That's the most concerning part, Headmaster. We went over all the shelves and documents in the room but we found nothing missing."

"Sigh, well if you have nothing else to report, then you may leave."

"Oh, there is one more thing that might be worth mentioning."

"Go on..."

"Out of all the enforcers that attempted to stop the intruder, there was only one who could land a hit on him."

"And who might that be?"

"The rookie."

"Thank you, you may be dismissed." And the captain left the room.

Left alone in his office, Headmaster Volice stared out of the window and into the sun. The last bit of information that the investigator gave him piqued his interest and gave him a slight clue as to who sent the intruder. "Things are about to get interesting." He uttered to himself.

It was now morning in Nadir, although it was difficult to tell with most of the light being blocked out. Myla happened to wake up on her own today. As she stretched to get ready for the day, she realized that it was far too quiet. Normally, Sahil would have been out in the halls waking up everyone with his pots and pans. Thinking it was strange, she quickly rolled out of bed and got ready to get to the dining hall.

There was nothing majestic about the dining halls either but it was better kept than most of the other structures and places in Nadir. It was filled with wooden tables and chairs throughout but no one was there. Again, Myla thought this was peculiar as this place would normally be booming with people during breakfast hours.

"Where could everyone be?" She heard a noise from outside the inn and she went to examine what was causing it.

A crowd formed around two people who were the focus of attention. One was the girl who ventured out into the Polluted Wilds and the other was the gatekeeper of Nadir.

"Please someone, anyone! I need your help!"

"Absolutely not. It is far too dangerous and I will not allow it."

The girl tried to run to other people for help but the gatekeeper put her in a bind and restricted her movement. She was yelling while trying to break free but everyone stood watching.

Myla began making her way through the multitude of civilians. When she got to the front she saw the familiar girl from back at the store but now she was being held down by someone stronger.

"Hey, what is going on here? You shouldn't be picking on someone smaller than you!" Myla accused the gatekeeper.

"Stay out of this. This is none of your business."

His voice was stern but Myla couldn't look away from Amrita who needed her help. She jumped on the gatekeeper and distracted him enough to weaken his grip, allowing the girl to run away and hide. After seeing the girl flee, Myla was relieved but the man grabbed her by the collar and threw her aside.

Myla quickly got back on her feet and now she was staring at the gatekeeper on the other side. She got herself into fighting position, ready to engage in battle against a taller opponent. The crowd was all excited for the possibility of a showdown, but suddenly Sahil jumped in between the two combatants.

"Alright alright cut it out! There will be no fighting near my inn unless either of you are willing to pay for the damages."

The gatekeeper lowered his guard. "Tch, whatever. It's not like anyone is going to help that girl out anyway." He then turned his back and left the area.

After the anticipated fight was cancelled, the crowd began to disperse. As the area cleared, Myla could see Amrita was still trying to ask people for help. Feeling empathy for her situation, she brought the girl to one of the dining tables inside the inn.

When the food arrived at their table, Amrita grabbed a bunch and began scoffing the food down at an incredible rate.

"You have quite the appetite. Especially for someone your size."

"Heb quib jubging tbe wayb I eab." She replied with a full mouth.

"Haha okay just slow down and chew your food." Myla gave her some time to eat in silence before asking her a question that had been on her mind. "So where is your friend? I remember seeing her when I bumped into you the other night."

Suddenly, Amrita lost her appetite and the expression on her face switched. Myla apologized if she said something to offend her but Amrita let her know it was fine. She took a bit of time to gather her thoughts before sharing what happened that night.

She retold the events of what happened to her and Sissi out in the Polluted Wilds. Amrita had dragged Sissi along for a 'fun adventure' during the night. She wanted to prove how cunning she was by sneaking pass the gate and how brave she was by wandering out into the wilds during the dark. Sissi was always hesitant but she couldn't say no to her friend. All was going well until the wailing sounds began. Then a creature appeared out of nowhere and had its gaze fixed upon them. Both the girls attempted to escape together but after a short run, Sissi slipped and was apprehended by the creature. Amrita watched in horror as her friend was taken away but it gave her the chance to escape and return to Nadir.

"After I came back, I began to ask anyone in the town if they could help me find Sissi. No one I asked said yes, and worst of all, that gatekeeper found out I escaped and began scolding me in front of everyone."

Seeing how sad the girl was, Myla patted her head in hopes of making Amirta feel better but then she got a thought.

"Wait... you can go save my friend Sissi!"

"I... uhhh... I don't know if I can..." Myla hesitated.

"Please!"

"It's not that simple. I'm not even sure I can..."

As Myla looked back she saw that Amrita had fallen asleep on the table. She called Sahil over and together they helped get the girl up into Myla's room. Once they placed her on Myla's bed, they closed the door and left her alone.

"Thanks, Sahil, that's twice I owe you for today."

"Oh? When was the other time?"

"When you stopped the fight between me and that gatekeeper earlier. That was very kind of you to make sure I didn't get hurt!"

"Don't get the wrong idea. I just didn't want to go looking for a new tenant."

"WHAT?! Are you saying I would lose to that bully?!"

"I did not say such a thing."

"Come over here and I'll show you how I got the highest score on that training dummy!"

There was a brief pause for a moment as Sahil's tone turned a bit more serious. "So are you going through with her request?"

"Oh to help find Amrita's friend? No. Maybe." Myla replied unconvincingly.

"Sigh, I knew this might be the case. Guess I better start looking for a new tenant now."

"Wow, thanks for the vote of confidence."

"Don't mention it. Now if you will excuse me, I have to leave. If I stay around any longer I might become as irrational as you."

"Just tell me one thing before you go."

"What did you want to know?"

"The name of the gatekeeper. Who is he?"

"His name is Jacob."

Examination Day / The Gatekeeper

A typical day at Diamondvale involved six blocks of classes with recess and lunch in between. The classes are spread out between History + Theory, Geode-stone Technology, Combat Training, Geode-stone Experimentation, Endurance Training, and Mathematics. These were the classes that a student must show proficiency at their rank before being considered for the next level.

Today was a special day in Diamondvale, as most classes were cancelled to host an extraordinary event. Within the Ruby class, Professor Sam was preparing her students to before heading over to the function.

"Good morning class. I know you are all very excited to head over to the stadium but before we do that, I have a couple of important announcements to make. First off, I like to tell everyone that, we have a new student joining us today!"

The student introduced himself as Willyham. Many of the other students in the class acknowledged his presence by waving at him but they all had their minds preoccupied about today's exciting event. Sensing most of the students wouldn't be open to helping the new student out, Professor Sam brought Willyham to her most trusted pupil.

"Willyham, this is Netanya, our top student in Ruby class. She will be responsible for making you feel welcome. If you have any questions, don't hesitate to ask her!"

"Wait what? Professor Sam, what are you... You can't... PROFESSOR!"

"Oh look at the time, we got to get moving along!" Netanya was not amused as Professor Sam continued. "My second announcement is that will be another addition to the Ruby class family." She brought out a creature that looked like a lizard with somewhat goofy eyes and had Geode-stones coming out of its back.

"Everyone, this is Barmaan and he will be our new class pet!" When Sam finished, the class was cheering. "Now who wants to be the first in charge to take care of Barmaan?" Suddenly all the hands went down except for one.

"I'll do it!" Willyham shouts out with a big smile.

"What! No, what are you doing?" Netanya whispered.

"Way to take responsibility Willyham! I trust you will do an awesome job!"

As everyone was lining up to head towards the stadium, Willyham didn't think it would be fair to leave Barmaan all by himself in the classroom so he took the lizard with him. Everyone gathered up in a line and when Willyham reached the end, he was met with an unimpressed stare coming Netanya.

"What?" Willyham asked.

"Sigh, it's going to be a long day..."

The Headmaster sat in his private viewing area as he watched all the students and professors enter the stadium. He had much on his mind and was deep in thought until a couple of enforcers entered his room.

"Everything secured?" He asked the guards.

"Don't worry Headmaster, everything is under control. There is no way any intruders will show up today!" Affirmed one of the enforcers.

"Very well. Tell them to commence with the examination." Once he gave the order, the two enforcers bowed and then left.

The stadium was packed with students that were barely able to contain their excitement. Willyham in particular was thrilled but there was a lot for him to take in and much he didn't know.

"So what's going on exactly? It's only my first day here and all of a sudden there's some crazy event that I don't know about." After Willyham asked the question, Netanya instantly had a jolt of energy and pushed her glasses up, ready to explain.

"Have no fear, I, Netanya, will provide you with all the information you need! Diamondvale has four divisions. They are ranked in this order from lowest to highest: Ruby, Sapphire, Emerald, and of course, the pinnacle, Diamond rank. Pretty much everyone starts as a Ruby rank except for a few exceptions.

Anyways, for you to rise in rank, not only must you be proficient academically for that level, but you must also be well-versed in a major skill such as engineering or combat. Then once you have met those requirements, you will be asked to take an examination in front of a group of professors who will judge to see if you are worthy to move on to the next rank."

"Oh, that makes sense. So I guess today's event has to do with this examination you were talking about?"

"That is correct!" Netanya confirmed.

"But they can't possibly do this for everyone who changes rank. That would be extremely inefficient."

"That's true! Most examinations are held in small rooms with only the professors watching the student who is taking the exam. The reason why this is such a big event is because the one who is being examined today has the chance to advance from Emerald to Diamond Rank. Something that hasn't happened in years."

"Who is the student who will be participating in the exam?"

"His name is Arnav, and he will be battling a low Diamond rank student."

Conveniently, right after she finished that sentence, the announcer spoke. "LADIES AND GENTLEMEN, I HOPE YOU ARE ALL EXCITED BECAUSE YOU ARE ABOUT TO WITNESS A SPECTACLE THAT HASN'T BEEN SEEN IN YEARS!" The crowd cheered.

"TODAY THE EMERALD-RANKED ARNAV WILL BE FACING OFF AGAINST ONE OF THE LOWER-RANKED DIAMOND STUDENTS. WILL HE BE UP FOR THE TASK? LET'S NOT WAIT ANY LONGER TO FIND OUT BECAUSE HERE HE COMES!"

Right on cue, the gate on one side of the arena opened and walking out was Arnav. The crowd roared as a majority of people were cheering for him. Despite the volume of the audience, Arnav somehow managed to stay focused as all his training in the past several months has led to this moment.

Once he was at the center of the arena, the applause slowly faded. The announcer then took over and was ready to let everyone know who Arnav would be facing off against. The announcer reached for the document and was preparing to read it.

"GET READY FOR THE FIGHT OF THE CENTURY, WOULD THE DIAMOND-RANKED STUDENT NAMED, HARSHITHA, PLEASE STEP FORWARD!"

When the name was spoken, a veil of confusion fell over everyone. The students all began to murmur to each other, wondering if a mistake had been made.

"That can't be who Arnav is supposed to fight!" Netanya blurted.

"What's wrong? I don't get it." Willyham replied.

"Harshitha isn't a low-ranking diamond student. She's in the TOP 3!"

"Oh. I guess he isn't going to win huh?"

Watching the event transpire from his office, Headmaster Volice slammed his fist against the wall. He finally figured out what the intruder tampered with and he was furious.

Then there was Arnav who was standing on the battlefield confused. He looked around to see if one of the professors or the Headmaster would show up. Although none of those people appeared on the battlefield someone did, it was Harshitha.

Evening was approaching as Myla made her way towards the gate. She was ready to take on the gatekeeper if he would stand in her way but when she arrived there was no one to be found.

"No one here eh? I figured he would be all talk and no show. I mean he was probably the one who let Amrita and Sissi slip through the other night."

After she finished speaking to herself, Jacob jumped out of hiding and lunged forward with his crystal spear. He had the pointed end just inches away from her face.

"Only a fool speaks without knowledge. I was not the one on gate watch that night those two snuck into the wilds. I will also give you a chance to turn back or else I will have to use force."

"I won't do that. There is someone out there who needs help. Let me through!"

Jacob refused to move as Myla expected. The Gatekeepers have a sworn oath to never let anyone into the 'Polluted Wilds.' Many who have ventured into the wilds, never returned so to ensure everyone's safety, the gatekeepers were created.

"Listen, no one said you had to do anything to help! Just let me go on my own! I can handle myself!"

"You are a foolish girl who knows nothing. Now, return to the city!"

"No."

"Then you leave me no choice."

Myla got into her fighting stance with her fists held up. Jacob whirls his spear around before pointing it directly to his opponent.

Judging from an objective standpoint, it was clear Jacob had the advantage. His weapon alone gave him extra range. However, Myla was not your average fighter as she was well-versed in close combat.

The battle commenced without either giving up a slight edge. Jacob used the reach of his weapon to keep Myla away but he couldn't land the decisive hit. Myla was dodging and looking for an opportunity to get close but Jacob kept his spacing well. Fatigue was starting to set in for both fighters so they took a moment to catch their breath.

"I still don't get why you won't let me go help Amrita!" Myla shouted as she was panting.

"You will never understand but my reason is clear." Jacob stood on his resolve.

"I'll help clear your mind right now!"

Myla immediately rushed and swung her kicks towards Jacob's chest. However, he reacted by swiping her aside with the shaft of his spear. Myla then landed on the ground with Jacob's weapon pointed at her.

"It's over."

"Yeah, for you!"

Myla kicked the spear out of Jacob's hands. It flew into the air and landed out of reach from Jacob. Without a weapon, Myla went in with a double kick before landing a roundhouse to send Jacob against the ground.

She thought the battle was over but Jacob got back on his feet. He didn't expect Myla to give him such a hard time and he gained a bit of respect for her. It was because of that he decided to share a bit about his story.

A couple years ago, before he became a gate guard, Jacob had a younger brother who he took care of. Having no one else to look over them, the two were forced to work together. Though they didn't always agree with each other, they respected one another and found ways to make things work.

One day, Jacob's brother got bored of Nadir and wanted to explore the 'Polluted Wilds.' Jacob was apprehensive to go but he couldn't stand his brother's nagging. He caved in and they went to explore the 'Polluted Wilds.'

The events that transpired next were forever entrenched in Jacob's mind. As he and his brother traversed into the wilds, they lost track of time and soon it became nightfall. That was when they heard a wailing sound before seeing a mysterious creature appear before their eyes.

Jacob grabbed his brother's hand hoping they could both escape together but his brother slipped. Jacob tried to turn back but it was too late, the monster had Jacob's brother in his clutches and that was the last he ever saw of him as Jacob ran back to Nadir.

From that day, Jacob chose to become a gatekeeper. Not wanting anyone to suffer the same fate as him and his brother, Jacob vowed that he would never let anyone wander into the 'Polluted Wilds' as long as he stood guard.

After hearing his story, Myla viewed Jacob from a different perspective. She attempted to speak with him but she stopped when she noticed Jacob pulling something out of his pocket. It was a Geode-stone and while Myla was too focused on listening to his story, he found the opportunity to regain his spear. He slammed the Geode-stone against his spear, causing lightning to surge out from it.

Myla immediately distanced herself after seeing the initial strike of Jacob's enhanced weapon. She was not prepared to face such an opponent but there was no turning back.

As Jacob kept swinging the spear, it released bolts of lightning, Myla was forced to dodge and keep her distance. She was waiting patiently for an opportunity to strike but Jacob was not leaving any opening. Still, Myla refused to quit but as fatigue set in, her movement slowed and Jacob was inches away from having the spear make contact with her body. But on that last attack, the impact sent Myla sliding against the ground.

While she was sliding, images of someone holding a lightning spear began to flash within her mind. They didn't last long and Myla was confused as to what she had seen. She wasn't sure where they came from but she realized it could be her only chance in this fight.

Seeing her lying on the ground, Jacob held his spear and was ready to launch a jolt of lightning, enough to paralyze Myla but keep her alive. As he was about to do so, Myla suddenly spun her legs around and surprised Jacob with a kick to his chest.

"Lucky shot."

"Ha, we'll see about that!"

Without hesitation, Jacob used the lightning from his weapon and attempted to trap Myla in it. Bolts of lightning launched right at Myla, but one at a time, she somehow sidestepped each attack. Her movement stunned Jacob as she eventually made her way within striking distance. She focused all her energy on her legs and she aimed her kick right at his head to end the match.

Unexpected Battle / Mysteries

A rnav looked to the other side of the battlefield, standing there was an opponent he was not expecting, Harshitha. Everyone inside the stadium stood confused as no one had any idea as to how to proceed.

"Hey Harshitha, I think there's been a mistake in the scheduling. I'm not supposed to fight you. We should wait for the facilitators and..." Before he could finish his sentence, Harshitha cast an arrow spell that landed inches away from Arnav's feet.

Harshitha's action drew a reaction from the crowd. Instead of walking away, she wanted the battle to commence.

"This is insane! Arnav won't accept the challenge. It's way too risky!" Netanya spoke to herself.

"I hope you have a really good doctor at this school!" Willyham exclaimed.

Returning to the battlefield, Arnav was still pondering. This was a day he had long waited for but his opponent was exponentially stronger than he had anticipated. He was caught in a cloud of confusion until his opponent shouted at him.

"HEY! What do you think you are doing?"

"Harshitha, I... uhhh I'm..."

"Listen, anyone watching in this stadium right now would want to be in the position you are in."

That was when a thought occurred in Arnav's mind. He remembered how rare of an opportunity he had to become a Diamond-ranked student.

"So are you going to squander your chance or take a hold of it? What is your choice?"

Those words triggered something within Arnav who had a different look in his eyes. He drew out his crystal weapons, a shield and sword, standing by for battle.

"LADIES AND GENTLEMEN! IT APPEARS WE ARE GOING TO BE IN FOR A REAL TREAT TODAY. BOTH CONTESTANTS HAVE DECIDED THEY ARE GOING TO BATTLE IT OUT. HOLD ON TO YOUR SEATS EVERYONE! THERE WILL BE SOME FIREWORKS IN THE AIR!"

"WOOHOO! Go Arnav! You can do it!" Ajay cheered.

When the cheering dissipated, Harshitha wasted no time and revealed her weapon, a crystal orb. Her weapon amplifies all the magic spells that she would cast and the first spell she used was summoning fire arrows towards Arnav. Quick to react, Arnav used his shield to block the incoming arrows.

Knowing defence wouldn't win this battle, Arnav attempted to move his shield out of the way in between Harshitha's attack but her recovery was far quicker than any opponent he had faced. Every time he thought he had an opening, Harshitha would cast more fire arrows and force him to hold his shield.

However, he refused to panic. He took a deep breath and exhaled before starting to count in his head. Harshitha didn't let up her assault as she launched a fireball right at Arnav. The crowd was beginning to lose interest in the one-sided fight but Arnav was about to turn the tide. Suddenly, he threw his sword at the sorceress, but Harshitha dodged the attack with ease.

"Way too predictable. Now you threw away your only way to attack and..." But she spoke too soon as Arnav charged in and was about to slam his shield against her.

Arnav thought he had a perfect hit lined up, but Harshitha reacted by casting a wind gust beneath her feet. The wind caused Arnav's movement to slow down, allowing Harshitha to dodge the devastating attack from landing.

Harshitha regained her stance, while Arnav was able to retrieve his sword to fight another round.

"Hm, not bad. You were counting how long of a delay there would be between my attacks weren't you?" Harshitha asked.

"Maybe. I'm just letting you know you probably shouldn't rely on your fire spells anymore to win."

"Oh? Then let's put your theory to the test!"

She cast another fire spell but there was no immediate projectile coming from Harshitha this time. Instead, flames began to surround Arnav. The crowd watched in awe as Arnav was about to be surrounded by a cyclone of flame. The fires from the cyclone kept growing until it completely engulfed Arnav within.

The crowd awaited nervously as the smoke slowly began to clear. Ajay was hoping his friend Arnav was okay. "Come on Arnav, hang in there..."

Emerging out of the smoke was Arnav but his weapons no longer looked the same. His sword and shield had become enhanced as they were pulsing with power that could be felt by the entire stadium. Barmaan who was sitting near Willyham was startled by what happened. The crystals on his back suddenly lit up as they saw Arnav's display of power.

"Whoa, what is that?" Willyham asked as he was trying to calm down Barmaan.

"Geode-breaker..." Netanya answered.

"Geo-bla-who-ma-what?"

"Geode-breaker. It's a technique very few fighters can perform, usually by a Diamond rank. When pushed to their limit, a fighter can shatter the Geode-stone they possess and call forth an immense amount of power."

"Wow... Arnav must be strong."

"Yeah but..."

"Hey, what are you worried about?"

"That's a lot of power to control, I'm not sure if Arnav has mastered it."

"I'm sure he'll be fine..."

Harshitha was now staring at her opponent who had surprised her. She wasn't expecting him to be able to use such a technique so she was slightly impressed. "Well, you are full of surprises. Alright, let's see how you deal with..."

A blade beam nearly struck Harshitha as she was speaking mid-sentence but she avoided it in time. "Hey, let me at least finish talking, I was trying to..." Again she broke mid-sentence but this time it was because she saw the look in Arnav's eyes. His stare was completely blank indicating he wasn't in control of his powers.

Harshitha launched her volley of fire arrows in an attempt to slow Arnav down but his shield easily deflected the arrows away. He then swung his sword wildly and the gale force created from it was giving Harshitha a difficult time. As she was struggling to move, she saw Arnav suddenly appear with his sword in front of her and this time she barely escaped the heavy swing as some of her hair was cut off.

Seeing Arnav turning the tide of battle, the crowd began cheering for him. But as his aura became unstable, his power was beginning to put everyone in danger.

Security began to pour in to help settle the crowd and take control of the situation. Unfortunately, they couldn't handle Arnav's immense aura either. Even the police officers were in danger as panic filled the entire arena.

Harshitha looked around and saw everyone at risk of Arnav's uncontrollable power. She looked to her Geode-stone and then back at Arnav. "I'm sorry, I didn't want to have to use this but you leave me no choice..." She was prepared to break her Geode-stone but she stopped when someone appeared between her and Arnav. It was the intruder from the other night.

Myla's kick was initially aimed at Jacob's head but she switched her target at the last second and went for his dominant arm. The force of the kick was so powerful, it knocked the spear out of Jacob's hands. There was also a bone crack that could be heard from his arm.

Jacob could still stand but without the use of his dominant arm, he would barely be in fighting condition. Knowing Myla could have landed a lethal strike against him but chose not to, he decided to concede. He found a spot where he could sit down and tend to his arm. Myla began walking to the gatekeeper to see the severity of his injuries.

"Don't worry about me. I have been through far worse than this. But tell me, how were you able to dodge my attack?" Jacob asked with curiosity.

"I, uh, I'm not sure myself. My body sort of just reacted by itself, I felt like I've seen your attacks before."

"What? That is pure nonsense, I haven't shown that move to anyone!"

Myla shrugged in confusion.

"Whatever, take this path and then take a right at the fork in the road. That should take you to the Polluted Wilds."

She looked at the long road ahead and up in the sky as the sun was beginning to set. She took a deep breath before thanking the gatekeeper for his instructions.

"I still can't believe you are crazy enough to wander out there by yourself. Stay safe. You are a good person so don't do anything too rash."

Myla could see Jacob letting down his tough exterior a bit so she decided to ask more about the wilds. "Hey, I know it might be difficult but could you tell me more about the creature that appears during the night?"

"Honestly, I never saw the creature myself. The day my brother was taken, it was far too dark and my lantern was knocked out of my hands. All I remember was hearing that terrible wail before it appeared."

"Oh, thank you for that. I'll be on my way..."

"Hold on. There is one more thing I learned during my training on becoming a gatekeeper." Myla was all ears.

"As part of the initiation of becoming a gatekeeper, we had to learn the history of why our work existed. Security measures were put into place to prevent people from travelling past sundown because people were beginning to disappear."

"Was there any knowledge as to where the creature came from?"

"There hasn't been a clear answer but rumour has it that the creature didn't start appearing until a little boy ran off into the Polluted Wilds, crying and never returned."

"Crying? But what does that have to do with..." Myla was interrupted by a bell ringing noise.

"It appears the next gatekeeper is arriving."

"Wait what? But I still have questions!"

"Go now. If the other gatekeeper sees you here, he will not allow you to proceed."

Myla didn't have a choice as she gathered herself to head onwards. Before leaving she had a few last remarks.

"Hey I know this sounds crazy, but I think your brother is still out there." Upon hearing that, Jacob was stunned in silence. "I'll do everything I can to bring him back," Myla assured him.

"Thank you." He said with a grateful heart.

She turned around and made her way towards the Polluted Wilds. Right after she had disappeared, one of the gatekeepers who was scheduled to replace Jacob on duty appeared.

"Hey, Jacob! Anything to report from your watch?"

"Just the usual," Jacob replied as he looked into the distance.

Return of the Intruder / the Polluted Wilds

Headmaster Volice looked down from where he stood and witnessed the mass of chaos that was ensuing. The audience was in a state of panic, the enforcers were unable to take control of the situation. Arnav's power was uncontrollable and now the intruder that infiltrated their security a day before had returned.

He slammed his fist against the wall in frustration, leaving a giant crack against it. He knew it was time for him to take matters into his own hands before things were to escalate any further.

Back on the battlefield, Harshitha was trying to analyze her mysterious opponent. The only information she had to work with were the rumours she gathered of his break-in from yesterday. With nothing left to go on, she attempted to acquire more information.

"Hey! Who are you and what do you think you are doing?"

There was no reply from him. Instead, he turned his back towards her.

"Hey! Don't turn your back on me! I said..." Harshitha was so infuriated with the intruder for ignoring her that she didn't notice that Arnav was swinging his giant blade, causing a huge energy beam to head in her direction. She would have been struck by the attack but the intruder jumped in and pushed her aside.

She was picking herself up and getting ready to stop Arnav but as she was doing so, the intruder stuck out his hand. "Stay down."

"As if! I got this situation under control." She reached for her Geode-stone but when she tried to grab it, there was nothing there.

"Wait, where did it...?" She looked back at the intruder to find that he was holding her Geode-stone. "Give that back!"

As she lunged towards him to claim back her stone, the intruder pulled the stone further away in one hand but his other hand came in contact with Harshitha's shoulder and suddenly she began to feel light-headed and she fell unconscious. Now nothing was standing in between the intruder and Arnav.

Still, in his berserk state, Arnav began swinging his sword in hopes of hitting his target. The downward strike created a massive impact that shook the stadium. The intruder had a clear path to strike so Arnav instinctively raised his shield to defend himself. However, Arnav's opponent anticipated his move and jumped over the shield.

Once he was over, he landed behind his defenceless enemy. Arnav had no way to retaliate so the intruder pulled out a serum and injected it on the right deltoid of his body. After the injection was all gone, Arnav let out a warcry and his powers dissipated.

Everyone in the stadium was stunned by what they had witnessed. In mere minutes, one intruder made short work of a high diamond student and a top emerald student. Nearly everyone was quivering in fear, not knowing the invader's intentions.

He stood still but abruptly, he fell towards the ground. He was feeling an immense amount of pressure pushing down against him but he was confused as to what the source was.

The fear amongst the crowd was now starting to vanish as they saw Headmaster Volice had arrived. He was the reason the intruder was now contained.

"My apologies to everyone in Diamondvale for being late but have no fear. This intruder will no longer cause you any harm and will be punished severely for his crimes." The audience all cheered as their hero had saved them.

Then the enforcers appeared and all stood at attention, waiting for their orders.

"Take care of the two contestants and make sure they get the medical treatment they require. Direct everyone out of the stadium in a safe manner." After he gave the order, a majority of the enforcers took to their stations, but a small group stayed behind.

"What about the intruder, Headmaster?" One of them asked.

"Make sure he is detained. I will speak with him shortly."

S unlight had disappeared as nightfall had arrived. The only light source that Myla had was a lantern she was holding that allowed her to see within a four-foot radius. What made things worse was the air that surrounded the area. It was even heavier than the air in Nadir, making it harder to breathe.

Despite all that, Myla continued onwards until she came across a tree that caught her attention. She got closer to investigate and found strange dents and claw marks on it. Whatever made those were not from a creature Myla was familiar with.

She continued to study them further but she was so focused that she didn't notice something was behind her. Slowly, it made its way closer to her and then Myla felt something grab her shoulder. Instantly she felt a rush of fear. She was about to turn around and kick whatever it was but she stopped when she saw what appeared in the light.

"Amrita?!"

"Hi, Myla."

"What are you doing out here? Don't you remember the last time you were out here? Also, how did you get by the gatekeeper?!"

"That's a lot of questions. I'll just answer the last one. Jacob wasn't on guard duty anymore so it was quite easy to sneak past the other guy!"

"I'm taking you back, it is way too dangerous out here!"

"Hey! I managed to get back to town last time I was here!"

"That was all luck! You can't keep taking chances like that!"

Their voices travelled further into the woods and something lurking within heard them. Interrupting their argument was a wailing sound that Amrita recognized.

They heard a rumbling noise heading their way and they saw a shadow that leaped into the air and landed heavily a few meters away from them. As it slowly stepped closer to the light, both Amrita and Myla could see a glimpse of what the creature looked like.

What they saw was no animal they had read about or encountered in their life. The creature before them could stand on two legs but its two arms were longer and muscular. It also seemed to have Geode-stones injected throughout its arms, shoulders and back.

"That's the monster!" Amrita shouted. "That's the monster that took Sissi!"

Myla took a moment to assess the situation. The creature was much larger than her, which meant she was no match in sheer force. She also had to worry about Amrita and the fact that her vision was limited.

"Amrita, take your lantern and get out of here. I'll hold this thing off for as long as I can."

"What?! I didn't come all the way here just to run away. I want to help!"

"And what exactly are you going to do?"

"I can be the decoy!"

The beast had its sight set on Myla but Amrita began waving her lantern obnoxiously and calling the creature names. Immediately the beast diverted its effort to chase after Amrita. Myla couldn't believe this was happening, but she had no time to be distracted as she needed to figure out how to stop the creature before Amrita was in danger.

Amrita was quick but the beast stored up energy in its limbs. In seconds, it launched itself and caught up with Amrita. It reached with one arm and closed its grip, thinking it had Amrita in its grasp but when it opened its palm, there was nothing there. In addition to

Amrita's speed, she was also quite shifty and managed to elude the monster's clutches.

With the monster confused, Myla jumped to its eye level. She spun in the air, winding up for a kick that she delivered right to the beast's face. Her kick was strong, but the creature shrugged off the minor sting from her attack. While Myla was still processing how tough the monster was, it swatted her to the ground.

"Myla!" Running to her side was Amrita.

"Don't worry, I'm fine. Just get out of here."

"I'm not leaving without you!"

Amrita looked around and she got Myla's lantern and threw it against the grass. That ignited a fire that spread and caused a bit of discomfort for the monster. They saw this as their chance to escape but appearing out of nowhere was another Geode-stone creature.

This one looked very different from the one they were battling against. In contrast, this one stood on two legs, was about the size of an average human. It also had crystals coming out of the head like hair. As it stared down the two humans, it dropped something on the ground that caught Amrita's attention.

"Those are... Sissi's glasses!" Amrita was about to charge at the new monster but Myla held her back. "What did you do to her?!" It only had one reply, "Doomedddddd..."

The creature began to release shards of crystals from her hair, targeting Amrita. She closed her eyes and braced for the attack but she never felt a thing. When Amrita opened her eyes, she saw Myla standing in front of her, taking all the sharp Geode-stones to her body.

Myla stood still for a moment before collapsing. Luckily Amrita reacted in time and caught her before she could hit the ground. She apologized to Myla for everything that had happened but Myla didn't blame her for anything. All she told Amrita to do was to run away and not turn back.

The effects of the shards were beginning to take effect. Myla's body was beginning to feel numb and her eyelids were growing heavy. The two creatures moved towards Myla but Amrita stood her ground. Without delay, the humanoid creature released a few more shards that got Amrita at the side of her neck. She immediately felt the effects and was unconscious within seconds.

Myla, who was still slightly conscious, could see the bigger creature grabbing a hold of Amrita. With every fibre in her body, she forced herself to move but to no avail. She watched as she was powerless to do anything to save her friend. However, before she fainted, she saw a flash of light that appeared between her and the creatures.

Myla's vision wasn't clear but what she thought she saw was a cyborg. The man still had most of his face intact, but the rest of his body was augmented. She saw the two creatures attempt to attack the cyborg but he held out his arm which transformed into a cannon. Out of it, a sound wave was unleashed that deterred the creatures from pursuing them. That was the last thing she saw before her eyes closed and her head fell lightly to the ground.

Recovery / The Guest

Opening his eyes, Arnav could see the ceiling with the lights on. He was still in a daze but he felt something licking his face. It was Barmaan and the sight of the creature made Arnav jump and woke up his whole body.

"Hey! He's waking up!" Willyham shouted.

"Huh? Who are you? And what's that creature doing in here?" He asked while holding his head.

"I'm Willyham, the new kid and this is Barmaan, the new pet in our class! Say hi Barmaan!" The lizard made an unimpressive growl.

"Arnav you are awake!"

"Ajay? How did I end up here?"

"You mean you don't remember?" Arnav shook his head at Ajay.

"Of course, he doesn't remember! He lost control of his powers!" Netanya interrupted.

'Lost control? No way that happened, I...'

"Could you keep it down over there? Some of us are trying to get some rest!" Across from Arnav was Harshitha who was lying on her hospital bed.

"Harshitha?! You are here too? What happened? As Arnav yelled, someone came barging in through the door.

"Who is causing such a loud ruckus in this hospital ward?!" The woman asked in a scary tone.

"'Pst, who is she?" Willyham whispered.

"She's one of the school doctors at Diamondvale, Doctor Ashima."

"Is she a good doctor?"

"Well..." Netanya hesitates.

The doctor looked around and caught the eye of the one she thought was responsible for the noise. "So it was you, Harshitha!"

"What? I was trying to tell them to be quiet!"

"Making excuses, I see. According to my records, you still require time to rest and heal. I can help with that!" As she finished, she pulled out a giant crystal hammer. "Meet my trusty HEALING HAMMER!"

"Is that thing really used for healing patients?" Willyham asked and looked at Netanya and Ajay but they were clueless.

"Wait, stop! Don't you dare!" Harshitha tried to scare the doctor away but Ashima slammed the hammer against the top of her head and Harshitha instantly went to sleep. Everyone who saw what happened had their jaws dropped wide open.

"So? Who else isn't feeling well?" Ashima asked while looking for the next victim. They were all quivering in fear but thankfully, someone entered into the room forcing Ashima to halt her actions. It was Headmaster Volice.

"Doctor Ashima! Just the person I've been looking for!"

"What could you possibly need my help with?" Her tone didn't sound very welcoming.

"Not me, but the nurses down in the other unit require your expertise. I think you better go to them before an emergency breaks loose."

"Sigh, good help is so hard to find these days." The Headmaster smiled in agreement.

Shortly after Ashima left the room, everyone felt a huge sense of relief.

"Phew, that was a close one!" Ajay said with gratitude.

"How is that person even a doctor?!" Wondered Willyham.

"Well, this is quite the unexpected crowd. It's quite rare to find students from different ranks spending time together. Oh and this little creature." He tried to reach out to pet Barmaan but he immediately ran behind Willyham.

"Sorry mister, I guess Barmaan thinks you are a scary guy." When Willyham made that comment, Netanya quickly rushed over to whisper to him.

"You dummy! That's the Headmaster of the school, Headmaster Volice!"

"Oh... OH! Hi Headmaster Volice!" Netanya facepalmed herself as Willyham just yelled out in the hospital.

"Haha! I like your enthusiasm! Oh, but I must not allow myself to get sidetracked." He turned his attention away from Willyham. "Arnav! How are you, my boy?"

"Physically I'm starting to heal, but I can't shake this uneasy feeling I have about what happened in the stadium. It's all a blur to me."

The Headmaster sat down and recounted the events that happened at the stadium. He spoke about how Arnav used the Geode-breaker technique and then lost control of his powers. That was when Arnav began to feel even more troubled. He was afraid of how many people he hurt, including Harshitha.

"Oh Arnav it's not your fault Harshitha is in the hospital right now," Ajay added.

"Huh? Then who managed to do that to her?!"

"There was this mysterious dude that showed up looking all calm and cool. He took you and your friend out pretty good..." Willyham chimed in.

"Mysterious dude? You don't mean, THE INTRUDER! Where is he now?"

"Hey, no need to worry Arnav! Headmaster Volice showed that guy who's boss!"

"Oh Ajay, you are far too kind!"

Arnav felt relieved after hearing that the intruder was taken care of but Netanya's curiosity had been piqued.

"So who is this mystery man?"

"I am not too sure myself Netanya, but don't worry, I'm sure the investigation team will have this all figured out. You don't need to get yourself involved!"

Netanya was not satisfied with his answer. She wanted to pry more information out of him but there was another knock on the door. It was one of the police enforcers wanting to speak with the Headmaster.

"Pardon me. That is my queue to take off. Stay safe everyone and stay out of trouble. Oh and get some rest, Arnav!" He left the room.

"Wow, Headmaster Volice is such a nice man. We are very lucky to have him!" Willyham said but Barmaan didn't share the same opinion. There was also Netanya, who wasn't buying his facade. She had a weird feeling about the headmaster that wouldn't go away but she kept it to herself.

Just outside of the room that Arnav and Harshitha were resting in, Headmaster Volice began walking away with his most trusted enforcer, the captain.

"Headmaster, there are reports that there have been trespassers spotted in the Polluted Wilds."

"Were they apprehended?"

"Not all I'm afraid."

"Sigh, it's getting too dangerous to leave those pesky Nadirians unchecked. I trust I can leave you with this task without further complicating matters?"

"Yes, Headmaster."

"Excellent."

Myla opened her eyes to find a makeshift blanket over her. She pulled herself up and suddenly remembered about her battle against the Geode-stone monsters. Immediately she looked around her body where all her wounds had been treated and bandaged up.

She felt a slight sense of relief and began to assess her whereabouts. It seemed she was in a small cavern. She wondered who it belonged to, and then her mind noticed something extremely important, Amrita was nowhere to be found.

Right as that happened, someone entered the cavern which startled her. It was the cyborg from back at the Polluted Wilds. "Oh, you are awake. Good, I can bring you to meet..."

The cyborg was interrupted as Myla threw a kick right at his face. Against most opponents, she would have knocked them out, but the mechanical armour protected the cyborg. He retaliated by grabbing her leg and then throwing her across the cave. However, Myla managed to reorient herself and land on her feet.

"What are you doing you crazy lady?!"

"Crazy?! You are the one who kidnapped me and Amrita!"

"I didn't kidnap anyone!"

"Oh yeah? Then prove it. If you aren't a kidnapper, show me my friend."

"I don't have her!"

Myla was done with talking. She pounced on the cyborg and grabbed onto his back. Knowing her typical fighting tactics weren't going to help against his tough armour, she resorted to a new strategy.

"What are you doing? Stop tampering with my systems!" He tried to shake her off but she hung on tight, trying to do all she could to sabotage his circuits.

"What does this do?" After pressing a button, the cyborg began to play some disco music while dancing.

"Hey don't touch that!"

"Oh, how about this one?" He suddenly bursted into opera.

"Quit it!"

"Oh oh, one more!" Then there was this button that turned him into a caretaker robot.

"Hi, I'm Bay..." The program cut out as he started to regain control. "Ok, that did it!"

He finally took control of the situation by grabbing Myla's arm when she wasn't paying attention and threw her against the ground. He then had her pinned and one of his arms turned into a cannon that was held right at Myla's face.

Myla was stuck in a bind but as she was struggling to break free, she suddenly had a memory of her and a human that had the same face as the cyborg. "What was that? How come it feels like I've seen this cyborg before?"

But before the situation could escalate further, someone called out. "That's enough Dante, that's no way to treat our guest."

Upon hearing that voice, the cyborg retracted his weapon and released his hold of Myla. Now that she was free to move, Myla got up and her temper had cooled off. She followed Dante to a place in the cavern where a man was sitting by himself enjoying some tea. When he saw that both Dante and Myla had arrived, he asked them both to have a seat and make themselves comfortable.

"So who are you and what do you want from me?" Myla asked after some awkward silence.

"Quick with the questions I see. Who I am matters not. As for your other questions, I don't want anything from you, but I have a feeling you want something from me."

Myla was flabbergasted by the cryptic man's response. She knew he was right, what she wanted from him were answers but he didn't seem to be in the giving mood. Thinking this was all just a waste of time, she stood up from her seat and was ready to leave.

"Are you planning to return to Nadir?"

"That's none of your business."

"You won't be safe there. He will send enforcers looking for you."

"Enforce what? Who is sending whom? You don't make any sense, crazy man!"

"Oh my, it appears you have forgotten."

"Okay... This is getting way too weird. I'm going to go now!"

She ran as fast as she could out of the caverns. Dante wanted to stop her but the cryptic man held the cyborg back.

"But we finally found her. If we let her get away now..."

"It's alright, give it some time. I have a feeling she will open up soon."

The Archives / Lion and Enforcer

L ocated within the campus of Diamondvale was the Archives, a place that possessed the greatest amount of knowledge in all of Zenith. If anyone wanted answers about the history of Zenith or to study any skill of their choice, this was the place to be. However, despite all the information available to everyone in Diamondvale, this place had a difficult time exceeding occupancy beyond twenty.

On this day, Netanya decided to enter into the Archives. She had a feeling what she wanted to look for would be difficult to find so she asked a librarian for assistance. She walked to the librarian's desk and tried to get his attention. The librarian didn't respond at first so she repeated what she said.

"Excuse me sir, but could you please help me?"

"Whoa!"

"Huh? What's wrong?"

"I'm sorry, it's just been so long since we had someone come to the Archives and ask us questions."

"Well, can you direct me to what I'm looking for?"

"Uh, yeah. What you are looking for should be on the last shelf at the back of the library."

Netanya thanked the awkward librarian for his help and she quickly made her way to the end of the library so she could avoid conversing further with him.

Netanya was filled with anticipation to find what she was looking for, but when she reached the end of the hall, her excitement had fled. Not only was the shelf the largest in the entire library, but it also wasn't well organized. Despite what seemed to be an insurmountable task, Netanya rolled up her sleeves and began searching for what she needed.

Time was flying by but Netanya was so enraptured in her frantic search that she hadn't noticed. She found countless information about the history of Diamondvale: the founders and all the headmasters in the past but none of the information was what she was looking for. So she continued flipping through a multitude of pages at a rapid rate. As she was focused on her task, someone behind her was about to reach out and grabbed her shoulder.

"AHHHHH!" She panicked but she was relieved when she saw who it was. "Ajay! Willyham!" She was quite loud so one of the librarians came to tell her to quiet down and Netanya felt so embarrassed as she apologized.

"What are you two doing here?" She said in a low-volume voice.

"That's a question I'm supposed to ask you. Nobody goes to the Archives! It's such a boring place to be!" Ajay replied without giving Willyham a chance to speak.

"Just leave me alone, I got work to do."

"Seriously Netanya, you aren't going to get out of Ruby class unless you get your head out of these books."

Ajay's last comment stung Netanya and caused her to go off. She lost her cool and blasted Ajay with a plethora of unkind words. Ajay was stunned in silence as he had never seen Netanya in this much rage before. While Netanya was still going off, Willyham noticed Barmaan walking towards one of the bookshelves and grabbed hold of him before he could escape further. He then noticed a book that Barmaan tried to pull out and opened it.

"Hey! You two used to be in the same class." Willyham raised his voice in excitement.

"Uh yeah... But how did you know that?" Netanya asked.

"It's right here in this book! Check it out!"

Ajay and Netanya both looked at the pictures. It brought them on a small trip down memory lane. While Ajay was still thinking about their past, Netanya noticed something off about the photo.

"Wait, something isn't right."

"What, you didn't comb your hair for photo day?" Ajay jested.

"No not that! The people in the class, they are..."

Before Netanya could finish her sentence, the librarian stepped in. "Unfortunately, due to multiple noise complaints, I will have to ask you all to leave."

Ajay and Willyham had no problem with the librarian's request as they were more than happy to leave. In contrast, Netanya was devastated, she needed more time to go over the information she had just acquired. The Librarian told Netanya she would be banned from the Archives for a week, so she snuck out the book Willyham showed her and agreed to leave.

A small group of enforcers were dispatched out of Zenith and nearing the arrival at Nadir. They could make it to their destination before nightfall but they didn't see the need to hurry. Instead, the commander made the executive choice to camp for the night and continue their journey in the morning.

There were four enforcers in this group and as the routine goes, someone has to go out and bring back supplies. Because Max was the newest member, he was automatically selected for the job. As Max walked out on his own, the other three enforcers gossiped behind his back.

"Hey, you think it's a good idea to leave him out there by himself?"

"What are you worried about?"

"I've heard stories about a terrifying lion out in these parts."

"Do you want to go with him then?"

"No, I'm good."

"Then keep your mouth shut!"

With the air being polluted and much denser here, Max made sure he had his gas mask fastened tightly before examining the area. When he completed his assessment, he began grabbing what he needed for a campfire.

After a few minutes had passed, Max was ready to return to the campsite. However, as he was about to depart, he heard footsteps heading his way. He hid in the bushes, not wanting to risk dealing with a dangerous animal.

Waiting patiently in the bushes, the footsteps grew louder and he could identify that those were the footsteps of a person. When the person walked closer in Max's direction, he got a clear look at the person's face. Max pulled up the report to check the photo of the suspect his group was sent out to arrest. To his surprise, the picture matched the person whom he was staring at. Without hesitation, he rose from the bush and attempted to arrest the woman.

"Halt! You are under arrest. Please remain silent so this process will be quick and painle..."

"WHOA! CREEPER ALERT! CREEPER ALERT!" Myla shouted.

"What? I'm not a creeper. I'm part of the police enforcers of Diamondvale!"

"Diamond what? I've never heard of that..." Before she could finish her sentence a headache appeared.

"Whether you heard the name or not is irrelevant. Now, remain still and accept your arrest or else." He pulled out his stun baton.

"Listen, I don't know who you think you are, but I'm not going anywhere with a stranger." She shook off her headache and was ready to fight.

They both stared each other down from the opposite ends of the battlefield. However, their focus was broken when they sensed an anomaly in the air. Something had been watching them for quite some time.

Pouncing from the bushes was a crystalized lion filled with rage. As it was in midair, Max and Myla jumped out of the way as the lion made a massive impact on the ground. After missing its preemptive strike, it turned to look at the two fighters and gave a ferocious roar.

Both Max and Myla knew it would be foolish to continue their fight in their current state. Instead, they had a temporary ceasefire to deal with a common enemy. They charged the lion together but their rhythm was out of sync.

Myla performed a flip kick that accidentally hit Max in the gut. She apologized but Max wasn't very impressed. He attempted to show her how it was done by swinging the electrical baton at the lion. Max also missed his attack but the lion retaliated by using its tail to whip Max's weapon out of his hand. It flew into the air and then landed against Myla's back, shocking her.

"Hey, whose side are you on?" Myla asked furiously.

"I don't want to hear that from you!"

They would have argued for longer but the lion refused to be ignored. It let out another roar, provoking the two to attack. Max had enough, he told Myla to stay out of his way and he charged recklessly towards the lion. Again he swung his weapon at the beast but this time his foe didn't dodge the attack. Instead, the lion used its claw and swiped Max.

Myla grew worried as she saw the lion's claw make contact with Max's upper body. Luckily, Max had armour on which protected his torso. However, the claws of the lions were sharp and they sliced through the mask that was covering his face.

With his face revealed, Myla had another headache. Her brain was trying desperately to show her a memory but she couldn't understand what was happening. All she knew was her instinct telling her to save the enforcer who wanted to arrest her.

Max was lying on his back, struggling to get up but the lion prevented him from doing so by pouncing on him. The lion opened its mighty jaw but Max was quick to react. Using his baton, he prevented the lion from closing its jaw temporarily.

However, the baton would eventually snap and then he would be vulnerable to the lion. That's when Myla performed a jump kick that knocked the lion out of the way. Max was slow to get up but he could hear Myla shouting at him.

"Stop taking your sweet time and get out of here!"

Knowing he was in no condition to fight, Max walked away from the battlefield and left Myla alone. Once the enforcer was out of sight, Myla was completely focus on her opponent. All the training she put in was starting to shine in this battle.

When the lion swipes at her with its claw, Myla weaves under its arm and then counters by kneeing the lion in the ribs. She repeated this pattern and over time, the lion's stamina was beginning to drain out. With its movement slowing down, Myla sensed now was the opportunity to land the finishing strike. She was about to throw a furious roundhouse but as she was in mid-kick, she saw a tag across the lion's collar. The first few characters seemed to be random numbers but the last three characters caught her attention: 'LEO'.

Upon seeing the tag, Myla froze, allowing the lion to swat her, slamming her against the ground. Myla attempted to get up but the lion was already standing above her with its jaws ready to attack. The lion lunged forward and Myla shielded herself with her arms.

The lion was within an inch of making contact with Myla but he never reached because an arrow landed on the weak side of the lion's limbs. Myla looked and standing behind was Max who had returned with a bow in his hand that he quickly put together with the resources in the forest.

Myla was surprised to see that Max had returned. She was about to thank him for saving her but the lion made a loud cry. It was limping as one of its legs was struck by Max's arrow and it was slowly trying to get away. However, Max had his bow up and his arrow drawn back, ready to fire.

"Hey! What are you doing?" Myla jumped in.

"Can't risk having this thing come back. It's too dangerous and has to be dealt with now!"

"You don't understand, I don't think this lion is what it seems to be."

"What? That makes no sense at all!" Max aimed his arrow at the lion but Myla blocked his way.

"Move or this arrow will have your name on it." Max threatened.

Myla stood her ground and because of her actions, the lion managed to escape into the forest. Max lost sight of his target and he put away his weapons.

"I hope you are happy. Now that lion will be able to roam free and harm others."

"I know this might sound weird, but I think that lion was once human."

"What? That's impossible. What kind of fool do you take me for?"

"I know it sounds absurd but..."

She wanted to explain herself further but she could hear other voices out in the distance. It was the other enforcers that were part of Max's group. He had been gone a long time and they were searching for him. It was upon hearing their voices that Max remembered that his main goal was to apprehend Myla.

Myla couldn't afford to remain in the area. She immediately fled the scene and returned to Nadir. After she left, the three enforcers emerged and found Max alone.

"Hey Max, we heard a terrifying roar coming from this area. What was that?" One of them asked.

"A Lion."

"Where is it?!" The other one asked.

"It got away."

"No way! You survived against the mythical lion of Nadir?! We underestimated you!"

Max didn't say anything but the commander of the group was a bit skeptical. "Private Max, other than the lion, do you have anything else to report?"

He paused for a moment before answering, "Nothing to report, sir."

Prisoner Visit / Search the Premise

After having a difficult sleep, Arnav woke up abruptly from his slumber, sweating and breathing heavily early in the morning. He wiped the sweat off his forehead with his arm as he tried to get over the nightmare he had. However, he wouldn't have much time to himself as his train of thought was interrupted.

"Seriously? Even in your sleep, you cause so much noise!" Harshitha complained.

"Oh sorry Harshitha, I forgot you were in the same unit as me."

"Ugh, now it's going to be so hard to fall back to sleep!"

"Hey, Harshitha?"

"What is it now?"

"Do you know where they keep prisoners in Diamondvale?"

"Huh? Why in the world would you want to know that?"

"Please, Harshitha."

"That's not a good enough reason. You ain't getting that information from me that easily."

"If you tell me it will allow me to be at peace and not disrupt your sleep ever again."

"It's in the coliseum. There is an underground access there somewhere."

"Thanks, Harshitha!"

With that, Arnav dashed out of his hospital bed and out of the room. Harshitha just shrugged her shoulders and went back to sleep. Arnav would return to his unit an hour later with some items that he had hidden in his bed. He would go about his day, listening to all the hospital protocols to help him rehabilitate his strength.

When nightfall appeared and the lights went out in his unit, Arnav stopped pretending to sleep and pulled out the items he snuck in. It was a change of clothes that would allow him to move stealthily through the school in the night. He left through the hospital window and then made his way to the coliseum.

As he was swiftly moving towards the coliseum, he was reminiscing about the nightmare he had. He kept seeing the masked intruder in all his visions. He wasn't doing anything to harm him but he was always present. Unable to block it out of his mind he had to find some answers and this seemed to be the best course of action.

Once he arrived at the coliseum, he surveyed the area in hopes of finding the entrance to the prison. He searched for some time but he could not find any trace. He was about to throw in the towel when he heard a noise coming from the distance. With the sound approaching, he hid behind cover.

Walking into the coliseum was a guard holding a Geode-stone as his light source. He made his way to the other side and then pressed a hidden switch that blended in with the walls. When activated, part of the wall moved aside revealing a wooden door that had a small opening in the top middle area. The guard did a very specific knock sequence before the door opened.

Leaving was the guard that was previously in the secret entrance and now he was switching out with the one that had just arrived. They exchanged places without a word to each other. Then the door closed and the wall covered the door.

Arnav saw everything that occurred, so he ran up to the wall to repeat every step. He pressed the button hidden on the wall, which revealed the door. He then mimicked the knocking sequence from what he heard earlier but then he realized his mistake.

Before the door opened, the door viewer slid open with a confused-sounding guard. "Hey, it's not time to switch yet. Huh? No one is here?" The guard thought it was strange, so he opened the door to see if he missed anything. Little did he know, Arnav was hanging on the ceiling above him, so he dropped down and tackled the guard to the ground.

Arnav then squeezed the shoulder of the guard, hoping it would put the guard in an unconscious state but nothing happened. "What? The intruder made it look so easy..." He thought to himself. With the guard struggling to break free, Arnav had to think of another way to immobilize the guard without causing him much harm. That was when he remembered, all the enforcers carry a stun baton.

He found the baton hoisted by the guard's hip and he activated the upper stun level on the weapon that wouldn't cause major harm to his body. Arnav pushed the baton against the guard's shoulder and in seconds, the guard fell unconscious. He then pulled the guard inside to clear up the scene of the crime.

Finally, he was free to explore the prison and find the mysterious intruder. Thankfully the place wasn't too big and there weren't many jail cells. That gave Arnav a bit of solace to know there wasn't a huge prison operation happening underneath Diamondvale.

After a couple of minutes, Arnav made it to the cell that contained the person he was looking for. He slowly walked up and clanked the bars to get the man's attention.

"A visitor? To whom do I owe the honour?" Asked the prisoner who hid his face in the dark.

"No more games. Tell me who you are and what you want."

"Just the response I thought you would give. You haven't changed."

"Why do you speak as if you know me?"

"Maybe I do. Who knows."

"STOP! Reveal yourself!"

Arnav's frustration peaked and he demanded the intruder step into the light to show his face. The intruder had a small laugh and then stepped forward where his identity could be seen. However, despite seeing his face, Arnav was still clueless as to who he was.

"You still don't have a clue who I am, do you?"

Arnav tried his best but nothing, he couldn't figure out who the prisoner was even though he could feel it within his soul that he had met this person before.

"It's okay. I didn't expect you to remember. He did a really good job altering your memories."

"Altering my memories? Wait, who are you talking about?"

"Even if I told you, you wouldn't believe me. I am a stranger to you after all." He started to turn his back to Arnav and walked back to his corner.

"No wait, I need to know! Tell me..." In mid-sentence, he heard a noise coming from the entrance.

"It appears our time is up. You better get going now, before you get caught."

"Before I go, at least tell me your name."

"Devan."

Barging into the jail was a unit of guards who were armed and ready to arrest the person who broke in. However, when they arrived, all they could find was Devan by himself, smiling. They searched the premises but never found anyone else.

Meanwhile, after he escaped through a secret pathway that Devan told him about, Arnav made his way back into the hospital unit and snuck himself into bed. He had so many questions in his head with one of them being: 'If Devan knew of a secret pathway, why hasn't he escaped already?' Nevertheless, he was too exhausted and he passed out on the bed.

Morning had arrived and it wasn't a very busy day at the inn. Sahil was cleaning a few glasses with a cloth on autopilot as he had done this so many times before. He snapped out of his routine cleaning when he saw Myla enter.

"Oh, you are back. Guess I can take off the vacant sign on your door."

"Please Sahil, not today."

"Sounds like someone had a rough adventure."

"You don't know the half of it. I just want to head up to my room for some peace and..."

Before she could finish her sentence, someone came barging into the inn. It was Jacob and he was looking for Myla.

"Oh hey Jacob, how's it going?" Myla casually asked.

"Since when did you two become friends?" Sahil questioned.

"Oh, it's a long story."

"Myla you have to hide, now!" Jacob demanded.

"Whoa whoa whoa, you can't just barge into my inn and tell people what to do!" Sahil stepped in.

"Sahil wait, let him speak."

"There are enforcers from Zenith out there looking for you. They are interrogating everyone in Nadir as we speak."

"What kind of trouble did you get yourself into this time...?" Sahil was unimpressed.

"Hey, it's not my fault trouble keeps looking for me!"

Jacob looked outside the window, "They are heading this way."

There was nowhere for Myla to escape so they were left with only one option. Sahil told Myla to run to her room and he would handle everything else. With no time to argue, Myla went up the stairs, away from the dining area.

The doors opened and entering Sahil's business were four masked enforcers sent from Zenith. They slowly walked towards Sahil who was acting normal and minding his own business. Jacob was sitting off to the side and keeping an eye on the situation in case he needed to intervene. Once they were near the counter, only the leader of the enforcers stepped up to speak with Sahil.

"Ahhh fine day here in Nadir gentlemen. How can I be of service?"

The leader slams a paper with a portrait drawing that looks similar to Myla. "The girl, where is she?"

"I'm sorry sir but you are going to have to elaborate."

"Don't play dumb. We got leads that this girl is staying here Mr. Innkeeper!"

"Hmm, have you considered that your information might be incorrect?"

The enforcer was unamused by Sahil's games. So he reacted in a way that caught him off guard. He turned around to his other three members and gave them a command. "Search the rooms."

Not wanting to seem suspicious, Sahil smiled and allowed the enforcers to search the area. However, underneath the counter, he was pushing a hidden button that would alert Myla that the enforcers were heading her way.

The three enforcers searched through the rooms while the leader stayed outside in case anyone tried to sneak away. There were a plethora of characters in each room: an opera singer in the shower, a narcissist who couldn't look away from his reflection, and even a person who collected spiders in jars.

After doing a thorough search of all the rooms, the enforcers reconvened and reported to their leader that there was no sign of the girl. Sahil smiled confidently as they couldn't find any results. The leader looked away as he couldn't stand to be seen in defeat. He was about to leave when one of his enforcers realized that there was still one room down the hall that they didn't check.

Suddenly, the expression on the leader's face changed and he was about to barge into the room himself but one of his soldiers stopped him. "I'll go." The enforcer entered the room and closed the door behind him. Everyone else awaited his return.

Once he was inside, he made sure the door was closed before he began his search. Right as he turned around, someone jumped on his back and punched him on the head.

"Who do you think you are invading my privacy?!"

"Hey stop it! I'm trying to help!"

"Yeah right, what do you take me for? Stupid?"

After much struggle, the enforcer's mask came off and when Myla saw that it was Max, she ceased all hostility and jumped off.

"It's you! The policeman from the forest!"

"Yes, I'm here to tell you that my boss and two other coworkers of mine are outside waiting to arrest you."

"So you are here to turn me into them! Well tough luck, I ain't going down without a fight."

"No, I'm not here to do that."

"Huh? But aren't those your orders? Wouldn't you get in trouble if you disobey?"

"I joined the enforcers to arrest criminals and psychopaths that would harm innocent people. I might not know you but just from what I have seen, you don't seem to fit that description. I can't bring myself to arrest someone innocent."

"Oh, thanks."

"I'm leaving now. Stay out of trouble."

"I keep telling everyone, I try but... Hey, wait, before you go, at least tell me your name."

"It's Max." He put on his mask before leaving the room.

"Max? Why does that name sound so familiar?" She holds her head as she feels a slight pain appearing.

Max returned outside the halls of the inn and shook his head to his commander. Frustrated, the leader stomped his way out and his enforcers followed soon after as they returned to Zenith.

Suspicion / Cyborg Visit

The sunlight shone through the window curtains and hit Arnav's face. Although he had a long night, it was very difficult to sleep with the sun's rays against his face. He stretched to get up but as he was doing so, he didn't realize he had an unexpected visitor.

"Headmaster Volice! I didn't see you there!"

"No apologies needed, I did make it over here unannounced after all."

"So what brings you here today? Just wanted to stop by and say hi?"

"No, today I have some questions for you."

Arnav had a sinking feeling in his gut but he did his best to hide it. "Uh, sure. I'm not sure how much help I will be but I will do my best!"

"Tell me, how are you feeling?"

"Oh, I'm doing better. Doctor Ashima thinks I will make a full recovery in a few more days."

"That's good news. Another question for you. What were you doing last night?"

The question caught Arnav off guard. "Uh, I was here resting of course."

Volice stood up from his seat. "And you swear you are telling the truth."

Arnav wanted to reply but he was feeling the intense pressure of the Headmaster staring down at him. He tried with all his might to say something but no words came out.

"He's telling the truth."

"Harshitha? And how would you know? You were asleep." Volice wasn't convinced.

"Normally that would be the case. However, this guy snores so loud that it's impossible to get any sleep!"

"Hmm, I suppose that is quite the issue."

"Haha... sorry Harshitha. I'll try not to snore as loudly next time." He laughed nervously.

"I apologize for the interrogation Arnav, I didn't mean to intrude on your rest. You take care now." He left the hospital room.

When the door closed, Arnav let out a huge sigh of relief. "Thanks, Harshitha, you bailed me out."

"Save it. You are going to tell me where you were last night and what you were up to."

Unlike the headmaster, Arnav felt he could trust Harshitha. He shared the events that took place at the prison and revealed what he found out last night.

It was another quiet day in the Archives of Diamondvale, where there were more librarians than students. There was no sign that it was going to be anything different until a loud noise echoed through the halls. It was the fire alarm that sounded and everyone inside immediately evacuated the area.

As people were leaving, one student was waiting nearby for the perfect chance to sneak into the Archives, Netanya. She was the one responsible for causing the fire alarm to go off. Earlier, she set a stack of paper on fire and put it near a garbage bin just outside the Archives.

Once someone saw the smokey garbage bin, they pulled the alarm and everything went according to Netanya's plan. As everyone left the Archives temporarily, she snuck in without anyone noticing her.

Netanya returned to the Archives because of the information she uncovered the other night. Inside the book she stole, there was a list of students in her class from previous years who had vanished without any trace or explanation. She was determined to get to the bottom of this mystery.

She approached the front desk to locate the information she needed. After obtaining that, she went to the area of the Archives to grab the books that contained what she wanted. Knowing time was of the essence, she wasted no time and grabbed the three books she needed.

She was ready to leave, but that would prove to be complicated as the fire had spread and was now blocking her exit. She could hear the fire containment unit on its way but she could not afford to be caught. She turned back into the Archives hoping to find another way out.

She looked around but the fumes were getting worse. If she didn't find an exit soon, she would collapse. She was reluctant to use it, but now was the time to pull out her crystal wand. Netanya wasn't well-versed in combat but she had a high aptitude in magic.

She was about to cast a spell but her glasses began fogging up and she was coughing profusely. Her glasses fell off as she cast her spell against the wall. A hole was blown in the wall, creating an exit for Netanya. Once she was on the other side, she used another spell to repair the wall, allowing her to flee the area before anyone caught wind of her presence.

The fire at the Archives would be contained with very minor damage. The containment unit did a fine job handling the situation but they also had to file a report on the cause of the fire. One of the members who was looking for clues, stumbled upon a pair of broken glasses.

It felt like things were beginning to calm down after a series of exciting events. Myla had returned to her gym, sparring against the training robot. She was hoping a good workout would clear her mind but it didn't work. There were still so many questions in her mind and so many mysteries that she had no answers to.

She continued beating up the robot mindlessly, and in doing so, achieved another high score but she didn't feel any more satisfied. She was ready to leave her training session feeling empty until she heard the voice of someone she wasn't expecting.

"It looks like you need a tougher opponent." Dante challenged her and without question, she accepted.

As they were sparring against one another, Myla began to fire away what was on her mind.

"How did that guy you were with know the enforcers were after me? Why were the enforcers after me? What is going on?!" She grew increasingly aggressive with each question.

"Calm down. I know how you feel."

"How can you possibly know how I feel? You aren't even human!" That comment triggered Dante, causing his right arm to give a power punch that sent Myla slamming against the wall. She bounced right back and flew it with a jump kick that was blocked by Dante's mechanical arm.

"You are right, I'm not fully human anymore, but I've gone through what you are going through now. You feel lost and confused because nothing around you seems to make sense. You are seeing people you never met before but your soul is telling you otherwise, that you know these people somehow. You are being hunted down and you don't even know what you did wrong. You are questioning everything you know about your pre-existing life because everything that has happened recently doesn't add up but you can't explain why."

Not only was Myla speechless but she was shocked the cyborg was able to communicate how she felt. With her thoughts scattered, she lost focus on the fight. Dante grabbed her leg and then threw her on the ground but he restrained his strength.

Myla lay on the ground to allow her temper to subside. She realized there was no point in fighting against Dante any longer. At that moment, Dante let out his hand, and Myla accepted it. When they got up, they sat at opposite ends of the bench to continue their conversation.

"Hey, sorry I said those mean things earlier." Myla apologized.

"It's fine. I've heard worse. Way worse."

"How did you become a cyborg anyway?"

"Honestly, I don't know. All I remember is waking up in the middle of the forest alone. Wanting to grab some water, I moved to a river nearby where I saw my reflection. That was when I found out I was no longer fully human. At that moment, my anger took over and I was taking it out on everything around me. If left to my rampage I probably would have destroyed myself along with everything in my path."

"Then how did you get it under control?"

"A man in the forest saw me and instead of running away like most people, he approached me. Out of reaction, I was going to attack him but he somehow managed to freeze my entire movement. He could have easily defeated me and left me alone but instead, he took me in and taught me everything I know. I think he can help you too."

"Man in the forest? Wait! You can't be talking about that crazy man I saw from that day!"

"Yeah, that's him. His name is Rice."

"What kind of name is that?! Anyway, that is beside the point. How does this Rice guy plan to help me?"

"You want answers don't you?"

"Well yeah. Does he have any?"

"Yes, but he's probably not going to give them to you directly."

"Figures..."

"But he did mention, things will be more clear if you make your way to Zenith."

"To the upper city? That is way too dangerous."

"Says the person who was willing to go to the Polluted Wilds all alone."

"Okay fair point. But how are we going to get there? It's not like we have a map."

"Yes, we do."

"Where is this map of yours? I don't see it."

"I'm the map," Dante responded with confidence.

"Wait what?"

"I guess it's settled. We leave for Zenith first thing tomorrow morning. See you bright and early."

"Wait, I never agreed to..." But it was too late, Dante had already disappeared and Myla was left frustrated. She knew she didn't have another option to get her answers so she headed home to rest to prepare for her journey with the cyborg.

Fugitives / The Pirate

Headmaster Voice sat alone in his office with many thoughts going through his mind. The intruder at the coliseum, Arnav's suspicious activity, and hearing that some of the residents of Nadir were leaving their boundaries. He was having a difficult time but he was about to have more added to his plate.

There was a knock on his door and although he wasn't in the mood for interruptions, he allowed the person to enter. A man with a file folder walked up to the headmaster and reported the fire that happened at the Archives.

Voice thought it was strange for there to be a sudden fire at that location. He asked to look at the file and the man handed it to him. He quickly skimmed through the notes and then asked if there was anything else found at the scene. The man pulled out a pair of broken glasses and handed it to the headmaster.

He examined it carefully and felt it looked familiar. Then it dawned on him, the encounter he had back at the hospital unit. "Netanya." He thanked the investigator for his time and once the man left, he called for his enforcers to report to him immediately.

It had been a while since anyone had seen Netanya. Ajay thought it was strange, so he decided to visit her dorm. When he arrived, he knocked on the door several times before someone finally answered.

"Oh hey Ajay, how's it going?"

"Where have you been? It's been days and no one has seen or heard from you!"

"Shhh, keep it down. It's not going to make sense but let's not talk out here." She allowed Ajay inside and she closed the door.

Upon entering, Ajay was expecting to see many books scattered and when his eyes saw the scene, he was even more flabbergasted. Not only were there books but there were papers all over the place with notes and writings that he couldn't follow.

"Hey Netanya, I think you might have a problem."

"No Ajay, we have a problem."

"We? What part of this mess did I create?!"

"No, Ajay! Take a look at this. Remember this picture I was talking to you about back at the library?"

"Oh yeah, your hair is still messed up..."

"Ajay, focus! Look at the people in the photo!"

"There's you, me, Arnav, Harshitha, and... Wait, who are all these other people? I don't remember any of them."

"Finally you are starting to get it. Now it wouldn't be too out of the ordinary for a bunch of students to leave the school but I thought I would see if there were any significant events documented that would have made people leave. I found nothing."

"Oh, so what does that mean?"

"It means something happened to these people and someone doesn't want us to find out."

"So I'm guessing that's what you have been trying to figure out all this time?"

"Yup! One of the books I got provided me with information on students who were missing. It's just typical information like height, weight, eye colour, medical history, among other things, but there was one I thought might give us a bigger clue." She pointed at the student's profile to Ajay.

"Vihaan? Why him?"

"It says here, he was a scientist studying Geode-Stoneology."

"What? Is that a thing?!"

"This second book I got confirms it."

"Just because a book says it, it has to be true huh?"

"Yeah pretty much! Anyways, this book goes quite in detail about the study of the Geode-stones and what great potential they have."

"You mean the Geode-stones we use to power up our weapons?"

"Ajay, the Geode-stones do more than that. They help power the entire city of Zenith!"

"Oh right, I forgot about that."

Netanya shook her head at Ajay. While she took a glass of water to clear her throat, Ajay noticed there was one last book she hadn't mentioned yet. "What's this one about?"

"I haven't had time to look at that one yet. But it's supposed to be a research log of what Scientist Vihaan discovered while studying the Geode-stones."

"What are you waiting for? Let's see it!"

"Wow, I never thought you would be excited to see a book. Fine, let's..."

There was a knock on the door. Netanya wasn't sure who it could be so she went to answer it. While Netanya left, Ajay stayed and waited for her return.

When Netanya answered the door, she was met with a couple of enforcers who asked kindly where she had been and that many of the professors at Diamondvale had been worried. Netanya quickly apologized to them and let them know that her health was fine. The enforcers were relieved but they explained to Netanya that since she had been absent from her classes for an extended time without any explanation, she needed to report to the administrator's office.

She realized her mistake and agreed to follow the enforcers. The two enforcers allowed Netanya to take the lead and they were about to follow closely behind.

"You know what to do?"

"Yes, before she realizes we aren't going to the office, we will tie her up without anyone knowing."

"Headmaster Volice will be pleased."

The two enforcers were so busy discussing, that they didn't notice Ajay sneaking behind them and knocking both their heads against one another. The heavy collision caused them to faint.

Netanya turned back and was appalled by what she saw. "Ajay! What are you doing? You will be in serious trouble for this!"

"I overheard them talking. They were trying to arrest you and hand you over to Headmaster Volice."

"Oh. Thanks for saving me."

Although they managed to escape this time, both Netanya and Ajay knew it was no longer safe for them to remain in Diamondvale. They had to immediately leave the school or they would eventually be captured and put into prison. They were about to become runaway fugitives.

It was another day of business for Sahil at his inn. He was doing his usual routine of making sure everything was in order and presentable for new customers that were going to appear. Once the dining area was ready, he made his way toward the inn units.

He would give a knock on each door to signal the guests that morning had arrived. He made his way to the end, where Myla was staying but when he got to the door, he saw a note left behind for him.

"Sorry Sahil, I have to leave for something important. Not sure when I will be back. Thank you for understanding!"

"Sigh, guess it's time to look for new tenants!"

M eanwhile, Myla and Dante had since long left the town. Having walked for so long, Myla requested for them to take a short rest. Although Dante wasn't impressed with the idea, he agreed to do so anyway.

"So how far is Zenith?"

"That depends."

"On what?"

"How many breaks you take."

"HEY! ARE YOU CALLING ME LAZY?"

"We first have to reach the Amazon Borderlands. That will be the most difficult part and then it shouldn't be too tough to get to Zenith after that."

"Amazon Borderlands? What is there that makes it so...?" There was a sudden noise that began beeping. It was an alarm coming from Dante's systems.

"Break time is over. Let's get moving. Also, it's your turn to carry this." He chucked a bag of supplies over to her.

Dante went on ahead while Myla was still sitting on the ground. She looked at the bag that was about a fifth of her size, dreading how heavy it would be. She was about to reach for it when she saw a monkey that appeared in front of her.

"Awww, hey little guy, are you lost?" She reached out her hand to indicate she meant no harm. The monkey remained still and it looked as if it would accept her kindness but suddenly he whipped his tail right at her hand. Then, the monkey threw dirt in her eyes and Myla's vision was obstructed.

She rubbed her eyes to get the dirt away. "Argh! Stupid monkey, if I find you I'm going to..." Her eyes were now cleared but the monkey had disappeared. Unfortunately, that was not the only thing that was missing.

"DANTE!" She rushed up to the cyborg.

"Sigh, let me guess, you lost our bag of provisions."

"Yeah..." She sounded defeated.

Dante pressed a few buttons on his arm to trace the location of the item. "It isn't too far from here, let's go get it back."

"Huh, how did you...?"

"I placed a tracker in the provision bag, just in case something like this would happen."

The monkey didn't run off far as it handed over the bag to the person who gave him the command.

"Let's see what you got there." He took a look at the content but a horrendous odour was let out. "Sarmaan, that is disgusting! It's a bag full of manure!"

The monkey fell to the floor laughing, rolling around and holding its stomach. The pirate was not amused by the monkey's prank. He knew the furball was hiding the loot somewhere else and he intended to find it.

While the monkey was still laughing hysterically, the pirate grabbed its face and pulled it. The monkey was no pushover, so it fought back, whipping its tail to defend itself. They were at each other for minutes until a cannon beam was shot at the pirate's feet. Looking at where it came from, they saw the cyborg and the girl.

"That's the monkey that stole our supplies!" Myla shouted.

"Those items don't belong to you. Return it to us immediately you thief or else..." Dante threatened them with his cannon.

"THIEF? I'm not a thief. No no no. I am, A PIRATE! Liam the Pirate! And this is my rascal sidekick, Sarmaan!" When Sarmaan heard Liam's comment, he smacked him on the head. "Oww! What was that for?"

"Pirate, thief, same thing!" shouted Myla.

"NO! THEY ARE NOT THE SAME THING! YOU TAKE THAT BACK!"

"The only thing I'm taking back is the stuff that you stole!"

Myla was about to rush in and jump toward Liam and Sarmaan. She was so focused she didn't notice a trap that was set, but Dante did. He jumped in and pushed her away just as a barrel near them detonated. Dante gave Myla a dirty look while she nervously apologized.

After her mistake, Dante used his scanners which revealed all of the pirate's hidden gimmicks. He avoided all of them and jumped up, meeting the pirate where he stood. Liam was caught off guard with the cyborg standing right before him. Dante was about to grab the pirate but the monkey jumped on the back of the cyborg's head and started messing with his circuits.

With Dante preoccupied by Sarmaan, Myla chased after Liam who escaped further into his hideout. As Myla appeared in another room, she saw the pirate standing on an elevated platform with nothing else around him. She learned her lesson and expected the entire place to be laced with traps.

"You want the bag back? Well, you have to catch me first!" Liam provoked.

She couldn't resist his taunt, so she took her first step forward and right away, that was a mine. Liam was throwing his arms up in celebration but when the smoke cleared, he saw that although Myla was hurt, she was still standing.

"What?! That is preposterous!" He exclaimed.

Myla dusted off her bruises and then raced to her opponent again. She activated a trip-wire where a couple of barrels dropped down on her and were about to explode. Without the slightest bit of hesitation, she rolled over to avoid the first and then jumped up to kick the other barrel away. The barrels exploded away from her and she continued pursuing the pirate.

"This girl is crazy! I'm getting out of here!"

Liam made a run for it, but Myla refused to let him escape. She dashed towards him and closed the distance between them. However, the pirate had another trick up his sleeve. With Myla going at high speed, Liam placed a banana peel between them and she slipped on it.

Seeing Myla out of control, Liam began to laugh. "Haha! You fell for the oldest trick in the book! Now I'm, oof!" As he was bragging, he didn't notice that Myla somehow crashed into him. Together they slid on the ground until they collided against the wall.

After the collision, it appeared Liam took the heavier impact and was still lying on the ground. In contrast, Myla was starting to get up and she held Liam by the collar of his shirt in one hand and her fist in the other. Myla had every intention of interrogating the thieving pirate until she heard noises a bit further from where she was standing.

She momentarily dropped the pirate on the ground and went to inspect what made the noise. When she reached the area where the sound came from, she couldn't believe what she saw.

Monkey Business / Pursuit

S armaan was climbing up on Dante's head and messing up with his circuits. However, Dante managed to grab the monkey and throw him away to create some separation. Sarmaan landed on his feet as they stood on the opposite side of the battleground.

Dante's systems analysis gave a normal status report, showing nothing peculiar about the monkey. However, from his tiny bout against the troublesome animal, he knew his sensors weren't picking up on something.

Using his rocket boost, Dante hoped to grab the monkey before he could react but Sarmaan was extremely agile. He jumped out of the way and then climbed to higher ground where he distanced himself from his enemy.

Dante then used his extended arm mechanism to grab the monkey. As his arm reached out, Sarmaan waited patiently until the hand was close enough to grab him. Right as the palm opened Sarmaan ran through it and sprinted towards Dante on the cyborg's extended arm. When the monkey reached the cyborg's face, he kicked the cyborg in rapid succession before landing a monkey drop kick.

After that surprise manoeuvre, Dante was shaken up but he took a deep breath in and regained some composure. Meanwhile, Sarmaan continually pointed and laughed at his opponent, which made the cyborg angry. He recalibrated his systems and then transformed his arm into a cannon.

He began firing at will, and Sarmaan was dodging them effortlessly. The monkey felt as if Dante wasn't trying and began taunting him by making goofy faces. However, when he saw Dante smiling back, the monkey looked around the battlefield.

There was nothing left but an open space. Dante strategically took out all the obstacles in the room, meaning there was nowhere left to hide. "Sorry, you are out of options."

Despite the change, the shifty critter refused to quit, as he ran in the opposite direction. Without much worry, Dante slowly went after the monkey, intending to trap him. The monkey scurried until it hit a corner in the room. He then reached its arm through a hole in the wall.

"If you return our supplies, I'll leave you be." The monkey replied by sticking his tongue out. After that response, Dante had no regrets about his next action. He directed his cannon at the monkey and fired a light concussive blast. He was trying to immobilize the monkey but when the smoke cleared, Dante found Sarmaan still conscious and holding something in his hands.

"No, is that a Geo..."

Sarmaan cracked the Geode-stone and a rush of power surged through the monkey's body. A transformation occurred as there was no longer a little monkey. Instead, a full-grown gorilla took his place.

"I was wondering how you were able to carry the bag of supplies all by yourself."

Dante attempted to acquire new information on his opponent's new form with his scanner but Sarmaan would not allow it. After squatting his legs, the gorilla launched himself forward with a burst of speed and tackled the cyborg, slamming him against the wall. Then Sarmaan found a slab of rock and with both hands, he flung it where the cyborg crashed.

The rock was thrown with incredible velocity but Dante managed to recover enough to see the projectile heading his way. He responded by disintegrating the rock with his cannon.

Dante now had an idea of his opponent's strength. He realized restraining himself would not be wise. With a press of a button, a voice in his system spoke. "Power suppressors disengaged." Dante was about to fight at full strength.

Sarmaan and Dante charged at one another and they clashed with their hands locked together. The two combatants were giving it their all, with neither surrendering the edge. As they struggled, Dante's systems were beginning to overload because of the sheer force. However, as his system was short-circuiting, his human mind began to bring out memories.

He was suddenly having flashbacks of a similar moment, only he wasn't battling a gorilla but an actual person. Every move the gorilla made was the same as the person in Dante's memory. The only problem was that Dante couldn't figure out the person in his memory.

Suddenly, he snapped back into reality as his system was alerting him, "Warning, systems malfunction imminent. Decrease power input immediately." Although he could hear the warning, he refused to listen and increased the power instead.

They both kicked each other simultaneously and as their shins clashed, they were knocked back a few feet. Sarmaan planted his hands and feet on the ground to prevent himself from further sliding. Then he launched himself right at his enemy.

Similarly, Dante used his boosters to stop his momentum from going backwards. Then he stored up as much power as he could and then shot forward right at his opponent.

With great fervour, the two fighters went all in for this attack hoping to land the deciding blow. Sarmaan swung his right fist as did Dante and they collided in the middle of the battlefield. The result saw Sarmaan's fist against Dante's face and Dante's mechanical fist against Sarmaan's face. Both successfully struck on their final attack and both had exhausted all their fighting energy.

Slowly their adrenaline gave out, and they were both about to fall onto the ground. Dante's systems were at the point of shutting down while Sarmaan was reverting to his monkey form. Before either of them could hit the ground, they were both caught. Dante by Myla, and Sarmaan by Liam.

Sarmaan had his eyes closed and was resting but Dante was still conscious and had a message for Myla.

"Myla, they are... they are not the enemy."

"I know."

Myla told Dante about what she saw when she was battling against Liam the pirate. After she slipped on the banana peel and collided with Liam, she was ready to beat the information out of the pirate to regain their belongings. However, before she could do so, she looked behind the pirate and saw that he was protecting some small injured animals. Momentarily, she had a vision of someone in the past who looked just like Liam taking care of rescued animals. Again, she couldn't pinpoint where she could have known the pirate from but at that moment, she had a feeling he was not a bad person. She also realized why he got Sarmaan to steal their supplies. It wasn't for them, it was for the animals.

"So you had it too," Dante spoke to Myla.

"Had what?"

"You had a memory of Liam, just like I had one about Sarmaan."

"Oh yeah, I did! But that's not the only time. I don't understand why it keeps happening!"

"The reason you keep having these flashbacks is because you know..." Suddenly Dante's voice faded away and he fell to the ground.

"Wait, finish what you were going to say!"

Myla thought Dante had fainted from exhaustion until she looked closely at the cyborg's neck that had skin instead of metal plating. Dante had been struck by a tranquilizer. She then looked at both Sarmaan and Liam and found they had been tagged on the neck as well.

She rose to her feet but before she could go into her fighting stance, a band of masked warriors wearing cloth armour, surrounded her. They each had a wide array of weapons and seemed well-trained. Myla normally wouldn't back down from any fight, but seeing that they had Liam, Sarmaan, and Dante all as their prisoner, she raised her hands to signal her surrender and followed the orders of the lead warrior.

After a bit over a week of rest, Arnav was released from the hospital. He just had to perform one last check-up with Doctor Ashima.

"Alright Arnav, if you pass this test then you will be allowed to leave the hospital. Are you ready?"

"Wait, you didn't even tell me what I'm doing."

"Alright! Here we go!" She pulled out her giant hammer and swung it without warning.

Arnav barely had time to defend himself so he took the hit from the hammer and was slammed against the wall. He managed to pick himself up from the rubble of the wall. As he was dusting himself off, he was anticipating Doctor Ashima to attack again but instead, she appeared with a clipboard.

"Are you feeling any broken bones anywhere?"

"Uhh, no."

"No headaches or feelings of nausea?"

"I guess not."

"Heart rate is good. Breathing checks out. Okay! You can leave my hospital now! Bye!" She signs off all the paperwork and disappears.

Arnav was left baffled by what had happened. That was the weirdest check-up he ever had but after getting that over with, he made his way back onto school grounds.

Exiting the hospital doors, he was ready to get back to training and his daily routines. Unfortunately, his excitement was doused when he noticed a warning on the bulletin board. There were two wanted posters for two of his friends, Netanya and Ajay.

"This can't be... What is going on? I have to find..." He felt a hand cover his mouth as he was pulled away from the public area and disappeared without a trace.

———————

Back in the headmaster's office, Voltce was sitting by himself, thinking about his next move until he heard a knock on his door. The captain of the enforcers had arrived to report to him and take on further orders.

"Headmaster, we attempted to speak with Arnav but he was released from the hospital today. We just missed him."

"Hmm, what impeccable timing. What of the other two?"

"We have sent a few of our forces to chase them down."

"See if you can track down Arnav as well. Having him run freely could cause problems."

"Understood headmaster." He then left the room to carry out the orders.

———————

Outside the school grounds of Diamondvale and into the streets of the great city Zenith was where Ajay and Netanya had escaped. Under normal circumstances, they would be able to walk the big streets and enjoy the festivities the city had to offer. But they were now considered fugitives of Diamondvale and were running through the alleys, being pursued by the enforcers.

"I can't believe they found us already! I thought we had a pretty good lead." Ajay complained.

"It's the bloodhounds, they can track our scent," Netanya replied.

Trailing behind them they could hear the sound of footsteps running and the bloodhounds barking. Ajay and Netanya kept running but when they turned a corner they were met with three enforcers that had cut them off.

Netanya was too hesitant and couldn't decide what to do but Ajay saw a large trash can near them. He quickly grabbed it and flung it at the enforcers, distracting them long enough to allow the two to escape. They were about to hit another corner but again there was a group of enforcers waiting for them.

They attempted to turn back but another squad of enforcers appeared leaving them trapped. The only place for them to go was the entrance to an abandoned building right before them.

"This way," Ajay yelled and Netanya quickly followed.

Once they were inside, the only place they could go was up. They ran up the stairs even though Netanya knew this was part of the enforcers' plan. The instant they hit the top floor of the building there would be nowhere else for them to run. She tried to come up with a plan that might get them out of this mess but while she was thinking, Ajay grabbed her arm, opened one of the doors and threw her in.

He then closed the door and smashed the lock to prevent it from opening. Ajay then made as much noise, running up the stairs to draw all the attention towards him.

Netanya picked herself up and as she was rubbing her sore back from being thrown, she rushed to the door in an attempt to open it. "Huh, it won't budge." She continuously tried but her efforts were in vain. "No! Ajay!"

Ajay had reached the top and for the moment he was alone. He took a deep breath to relieve his nerves and relax his breathing. Once he was calm, the enforcers had appeared on the roof.

In total, Ajay counted nine enforcers and three bloodhounds. Once he had a clear picture of what he was up against, he pulled out his weapons to face them. In both his hands were crystal hatchets.

The first to approach him was one of the bloodhounds that attempted to pounce on him but Ajay easily kicked the hound aside. Then two of the soldiers attacked Ajay with their stun batons. They swung the baton in unison and Ajay blocked each one with his hatchets. The two enforcers set out to overpower him but Ajay reduced his strength, and then using their momentum against them, he tripped both his enemies.

Three enemies were down but Ajay still had a long way to go. This time, one of the bloodhounds charged towards him with two other soldiers behind. Ajay evaded the bloodhound and went straight for the two enforcers. Their weapons clashed and were stuck in a deadlock. Ajay was ready to kick both his enemies aside but the bloodhound from earlier returned and bit his leg.

Despite being bitten, Ajay continued to fight on. He mustered all the strength he had and began spinning in a whirlwind formation with his hatchets out. All the rotational force was too much for the hound to handle so he was forced to let go. That left the two enforcers who were completely overpowered by Ajay's technique.

With four enforcers and two bloodhounds defeated, it looked as if Ajay had a chance at victory. Regrettably, one of the enforcers threw a canister right beneath Ajay's feet. Fumes were released from it which Ajay inhaled.

After inhaling some of the substance, Ajay's vision was now blurry and his reaction time was delayed. That left him vulnerable as three of the enforcers walked up to him with their stun batons. They alternated turns, hitting Ajay on the shoulders, back and legs.

Ajay did his best to endure the pain but it was too much. The fumes from earlier compounded with the shock of the batons. His strength was growing weaker by the second and eventually, his mind wouldn't be able to take it anymore as he fainted.

Seeing the former student of Diamondvale lying on the ground, the lead enforcers ordered his soldiers to cease their actions. They obeyed his command and were told to restrain their captive and make sure he couldn't escape. As they were about to carry their new order, they heard a strange sound near their area.

They looked to where the sound came from and they saw that their last bloodhound had fallen asleep. Suddenly the enforcers were on their guard, but as they were so focused on looking for their enemy, a canister rolled between them. This one created a large blanket of smoke around the whole rooftop.

The commander of the group was attempting to communicate with the rest of his squad but all he could hear were grunts. His soldiers were being attacked in the smoke. When the smoke cleared, the commander found two more of his enforcers lying on the ground with an arrow to their shoulders. He couldn't believe what was happening so he called for his last soldier to stay close to him.

That was when the leader was struck by an arrow and he began to feel dizzy. At that moment, he realized that his last soldier was the one who took out the rest of his squad. "You, traitor..." And he too fell to the ground, immobilized.

The last enforcer walked to Ajay and picked him up. He made his way down the stairs, to the entrance where he would find the other fugitive. The enforcer found the weak point in the door and busted it open. It was here that he was met with Netanya who held her wand, ready to defend herself.

"S-s-stay back! And uh, put my friend down! I'm not afraid to use this!" She sounded very nervous.

The enforcer slowly put Ajay down in a resting position. "Don't worry, I'm not your enemy."

"That's what the bad guy always says! I ain't falling for your tricks."

He then took off his mask. "If I wanted to arrest you, don't you think I would have already done that."

With his mask off, Netanya saw the face of someone she recognized. "It can't be, Max!"

The Amazonians / Break Free

Dante, Liam and Sarmaan were taken to an area away from where Myla was being led. She was by herself, wondering where the warriors were planning to take her. She thought of a prison cell but where they took her was a place she wasn't expecting.

The soldiers were all lined up perfectly and stood for attention as they put Myla at the center of the room. The warriors all chanted in unison before putting their weapons aside. Myla then looked to the front of the room where someone with an empowering aura, wearing battle armour was sitting on the throne. It was the queen of the Amazonians.

After seeing the queen, things began to make more sense to Myla. She realized why Dante, Liam, and Sarmaan were put into captivity while she was brought here. That also meant that all the warriors in this place were women.

One of the leaders of the Amazonians stepped up and bowed in the presence of the queen. Myla having no clue about their customs, was forced to kneel.

"Your Majesty, we bring news."

"Go on."

"During our patrol, we encountered an anomaly near our borders. We have arrested and put into custody three of the four captives. Two males, the other a monkey."

"And what of this one?"

"We weren't sure, your honour. That's why we brought her here for you to judge."

The queen rose from her throne and looked at Myla from a distance, not bothering to move closer. "Throw her with the others. One without manners is not welcomed here."

The leader was surprised by the queen's response. She was hoping she would at least test Myla's strength. She was about to take Myla away to the prisons when one of the warriors stood out of line.

"Your majesty, please reconsider your decision." The leader tried to tell her subordinate to be quiet but it was too late.

"Why am I not surprised that it would be you speaking up, Aria? Going against my word could be viewed as treason." Announced the Queen.

"I only have our people's best interest in mind. Our warriors have been battling tirelessly to protect everyone in the tribe. We have lost many comrades and there has been no end to our enemies' forces. Any help we can get, we should consider."

Tired of her back-talking, the queen walked down from her throne. All the other Amazon warriors continued to stand on guard but they could feel the tension that was in the room. Once the queen was directly in front of Aria, she spoke down to her. "I am the queen and my word is law."

The queen was waiting for Aria to say anything that would give her a reason to brand her as a traitor. Aria was biting her lip as she was hot-tempered and ready to let the queen know how she felt. However, before things could escalate, a soldier from the front lines rushed into the room.

"Your honour, I'm afraid I bring terrible news."

"What is it?" The queen replied in a disgruntled manner.

"Our warriors are doing their best to hold down the frontline but they need reinforcements!"

Immediately, the leader took charge of the situation before anyone else could speak. She told the forces within the throne room to rally to her. Together they were going to support their comrades on the frontline.

As the soldiers rushed out of the room in an orderly manner, the leader turned over to Aria. "She's your responsibility now. Give her a weapon and we'll see how she fares in combat."

Myla let out a sigh of relief. She was happy to know she wasn't going to be thrown in prison, at least not for the time being. However, the queen was still standing nearby and Myla could feel the animosity she had for her. Thankfully, Aria pulled her away. "Follow me."

Together they left the throne room and Aria guided Myla to the area where the Amazon would go to prepare for battle. Here there were assortments of weapons, armour, and other miscellaneous items.

"Hey, thanks for vouching for me earlier."

"Don't mention it." She was focused on finding the right weapon. "Here, how's this?" Aria showed Myla a sword.

"Oh, don't worry, I won't be needing that."

"Okay, suit yourself." She put the sword away and looked for something else.

"What about my friends? Are they going to be alright?"

"Oh, you mean the prisoners. They are alive for now, but I can't promise their safety."

"What?! What are you going to do to them!?"

"Not me, the queen..."

"Argh, why is she such a witch!"

"Haha, say that any louder and you might get thrown in the dungeon."

"Hey, I know you are thinking it too."

"Here put these on." Aria held out some war paint for Myla. She explained to her that every Amazonian gave herself markings as a tradition.

Not wanting to show disrespect for Aria, she took some paint and did as she was told.

"Don't worry. Your friends should be okay for a while. If you help us defend against the enemy, perhaps that will put the queen in better spirits."

"Alright, let's go get 'em!" And together they made their way to the battlefield.

Meanwhile, away from all the fighting, the queen had retreated to her room. Her head was aching and she was flustered by everything that had happened. She quickly sat down at her desk, grabbed the feather pen and began writing a note.

When the note was finished, she signed it off and rolled it up. She called for one of her hawks who had a harness to carry a message. Then she gave the bird specific instructions to whom the message was to be delivered.

As the hawk flew away, the queen attempted to relieve her headache by rubbing her head. "Sigh, he isn't going to be pleased knowing how close she is getting..."

Te atmosphere in Zenith had changed. What was once seen as a place of peace and solitude seemed like a thing of the distant past. With intruders appearing and fugitives being found amongst their people, the safety of the city has been up for question.

The enforcers were doing all they could to keep the public calm and restore order to the city. Their words were only bandages, not solutions to their problems. Sooner or later, they would need to provide results if they hope to have things back to normal in Zenith.

Hidden in an alleyway in Diamondvale, Arnav woke up and remembered that someone captured him the other day. Whoever that person was, must have brought him here. He was surprised to find out he wasn't tied up and then he heard a familiar voice.

"Hi Arnav!"

"Willyham?! Wait, where is your lizard friend?"

"Oh, Barmaan is taking a nap, back in his glass container in Professor Sam's classroom."

"I see. Wait... were you the one who kidnapped me here?!"

"Oh, I'm not strong enough to do that. Harshitha was the one who did it!"

"Harshitha? Where is she now?"

"Oh, she's over there." Willyham pointed and Arnav recognized the area. It was where they were keeping Devan.

Inside the prison, Devan was securely watched by one of the enforcers. The prisoner was lying on his back until he felt the need to speak.

"Hey guard, can I have a snack?"

"You just had lunch an hour ago!" The guard replied with an annoyed tone.

"I'm going to need a full stomach. After all, I plan on getting out of here today."

The guard was confused for a moment and then burst into laughter. "Wow, you are insane. There's no way you are leaving this prison!"

After the guard gave his statement, he felt a light tap on the shoulder. He turned around to see who it was. "Oh, you are Harshitha, the Diamond Ranked student. Phew, you scared me for a minute there..." Right as he said those words, Harshitha chopped him right at the neck and the guard fell unconscious. She then picked up the keys and slowly walked up to the cell that contained Devan.

"What kept you?" Devan asked.

"Give me one good reason why I should set you free."

"I like bargains! Well, let's see. I think you are going to need my help to escape this place."

"Your help with what? I can handle the enforcers."

"True, but what if the Headmaster appears." Devan's question had Harshitha silent. "Think you can beat him?"

She tried to ignore that possibility but she couldn't. Even though the chances weren't high, the fact that the headmaster could show up would make their chances of escape near zero without Devan. She moved closer to the prison cell and then there was a sudden 'click'.

"Thank you! You made a wise choice." Right as Devan showed his gratitude, Harshitha grabbed him by the shoulder.

"Give me any reason to think you will betray us..."

"Yeah yeah got it. Heard that one many times before. Let's get out of here." And they left the prison area and back out to ground level.

Back on the surface, Willyham and Arnav had their hands full as some enforcers had overheard their loud conversation. Arnav was more than capable of handling himself but Willyham was still new to combat. While Arnav was surrounded by a squad of enforcers, he heard Willyham yelling.

"Help Arnav help! They got me!" Two enforcers held him up like they were carrying a long piece of log.

"Hang on Willyham!"

Arnav quickly took out one of the enforcers with his shield, giving him an opening to go after Willyham's captive. When the enforcers saw Arnav getting near, they quickly threw their hostage away and passed him off to another pair of enforcers who caught him. It was like they were playing a game of hot potato.

With Willyham getting further away and Arnav growing more fatigued, it seemed there was only one option left. Arnav was about to pull out his Geode-stone but before he could do so Devan appeared between the two enforcers and took them out instantly. Devan grabbed Willyham and pulled him to safety.

A group of enforcers began charging in Arnav's direction but a firewall appeared before the oncoming enemies, immobilizing them temporarily. Arnav charged forward with his shield and bashed all the enforcers aside as he didn't want to injure them with his sword. Together, they dealt with all the enforcers in the area.

As Arnav was putting his weapons away, he could see Harshitha moving in his direction. "Hey Harshitha, Willyham said you were the one who brought me here." He then received a smack to the back of his head from the Diamond-ranked student. "What was that for?"

"You had one job! All you had to do was stay quiet and not draw the attention of the enforcers!"

"How was I supposed to know that?"

"Because Willyham told you." She turned to Willyham. "You did tell him didn't you?" Willyham smiled nervously. "Sigh..." Harshitha was not impressed in the slightest.

"Harshitha, Why did you bring me here?" Arnav asked.

"You are clueless, aren't you? You saw those wanted posters on the bulletin board didn't you?"

"Well yeah, but they weren't for me. They were for Netanya and Ajay."

"Suppose they couldn't find them, who do you think they would go searching for next?" That was the moment both Willyham and Arnav realized why Harshitha had pulled them away. She knew Headmaster Voice would search for them because they were connected to Netanya and Ajay.

"Then what about him? Did you have to break him out of prison?" Arnav was refering to Devan.

"Hey guys?" Willyham tried to get a word in but they continued their conversation.

"I have a name you know," Devan replied.

"Guys..." Willyham tried again.

"He's insurance. Just in case the worst possible happens." Harshitha answered.

"So what do we do now?"

"GUYS!"

Finally, Willyham got the attention of the other three. They asked him why he was trying so hard to interrupt them but when they looked to where he was pointing, they could see an army of enforcers running to their positions. They were going to be surrounded and although there was a chance they could win the fight, it would leave them too tired to escape from the school grounds.

"Quick everyone, into the prison now!" Devan shouted urgently.

"What! We just broke you out of jail and you want to go back?!" Willyham was in disbelief.

"No time to explain, just do as I say!"

Seeing no better option, Arnav and Harshitha made their way inside the prison. Willyham was still reluctant so Devan grabbed him by the back of his shirt and then kicked him inside. He then entered the prison himself and locked the door to prevent the enforcers from entering.

The door was shut tight and none of the enforcers could open it. Devan then busted the lock so the enemies couldn't enter even with their keys. They were going to need another strategy to get in and the captain of the enforcers happened to be there.

"Your group, grab the gasoline and spread it around the prison. Your team, prepare to light it up. I'll take care of the rest..."

Inside the prison, Harshitha, Arnav and Willyham were trying to think of a way to escape.

"Great, now we are stuck in this crummy prison because of you two!" Harshitha yelled.

"Us?! Who told you to go kidnapping people?! You could have just nicely told us!" Arnav responded.

While they were bickering, Willyham began smelling something funny in the air. "Uh, guys? Anyone smell that?"

"Hey, stop looking at me! I didn't do anything!" Arnav defended himself.

Not only was there a gaseous smell, but they were all starting to sweat from their foreheads. They also smelt smoke that was growing stronger by the second.

"Wait, gas, heat, smoke..." Arnav was piecing it together.

"WE HAVE TO GET OUT OF HERE NOW!"

Harshitha's voice signalled that they were in immediate danger. They all began searching for a way to break out. Despite their best effort, none of them found anything.

From the outside, the captain held the explosive agent in his hand. He threw it from a distance and when it came in contact with the flames, the whole prison exploded. He turned around and began to relay a message to one of his subordinates. "Tell the Headmaster that he has four fewer problems to worry about."

Geode-Mutants

J ust outside the Amazon's tribe, were cages to hold prisoners. Dante, Sarmaan and Liam each had their cage that they were locked into. Not a fan of being confined, Liam began making a ruckus on the metal bars.

"Hey! Let us out of here! I didn't do anything wrong!"

"Well, you stole our supplies," Dante informed him.

"Oh right. But other than that, I have done nothing wrong!" Despite his howling, the guards ignored him.

"Sigh, it's no use... Where in the world are we anyways?" Liam wondered.

"Well all these people that arrested us are female warriors. So I would assume that makes them Amazonians. Which means we are in their territory, the Amazon Borderlands." Dante answered.

"Oh, you are pretty smart."

"Helps when you have a computer to tell you."

"What? Thats cheating! Wait a minute... Couldn't your technology just get us out of here?"

"I think it would be wise if we let Myla straighten things out."

"What?! Who knows how long that will take? I don't think I can handle being here much longer!"

"It's only been one hour, you'll be fine."

Suddenly, Sarmaan began to act wildly in his tiny cage. He was letting out a monkey cry that was very difficult to ignore.

"Great, now your monkey is complaining too." Dante didn't sound pleased.

"Oh no, that's not good."

"Yeah, that noise is obnoxious."

"No, Sarmaan only makes that noise if he senses danger."

They heard some of the warriors on the outskirts under attack. Dante was hoping this wouldn't happen. He could no longer wait for Myla to resolve their dilemma. Dante yelled for the guard to let them free so they could help. Unfortunately, the woman refused to listen to him.

Shortly after, cries could be heard from some of the warriors. Their soldiers were falling in battle, but the guard refused to free the prisoners. The Amazonians were a proud race that stuck to their convictions.

The enemy had entered the prison grounds. They were creatures that stood on two legs with crystals infused through their entire body. Their face could hardly be seen and instead of hands, they had sharp crystal blades.

"What in the world are those things!?!" Liam yelled.

"Geode-mutants..." Dante said with a fearful tone.

"Say that again?"

"Geode-Mutants. They are mindless creatures that have lost their sanity but because of it, they have no understanding of pain or their limitations."

Standing between them and the Geode-Mutants was a small group of warriors. Together the warriors yelled their warcry and ran into battle. They looked to have the advantage early as the Geode-Mutants seemed slow and couldn't dodge a single attack. However, everything Dante said was true, despite taking those initial hits, the Geode-mutants got back up and continued to fight.

Slowly, the Geode-Mutants overpowered the Amazon fighters who had exhausted their energy. Three were lying on the ground and there was one warrior who could only lift her head and watch as her comrades were about to suffer a terrible fate.

"Hey! Amazonian lady!" Liam yelled to get her attention and she turned to look at him. "I know you don't want to set us free, but your comrades are in danger! Are you willing to protect your pride or will you let us help save them?"

She pounded the ground and came to a decision. With haste, she lunged forward and attacked one of the Geode-Mutants that was about to attack her comrades. She then grabbed the keys from her allies' belt and threw them towards Liam's cage.

The keys were high up in the air and Liam could see them heading towards him, but he couldn't catch them. The keys flew over his hands and landed away from Liam's range. "No! I was so close!"

The warrior saw what happened and she attempted to retrieve the key but one of the Geode-mutants tripped her. The Amazon warrior was about to be struck by the creature. Thankfully, a robotic arm appeared to intercept the attack. Dante had broken out of his cage and he grabbed the monster's arm and threw it as far as he could.

While this was happening, the key that was out of Liam's range was close enough for Sarmaan's tail to reach. Once he got the key, he unlocked his cage and then quickly helped free Liam.

"Well done Sarmaan, for once," Sarmaan replied by slapping him in the face with his tail.

"Oww, okay I'm sorry! Let's go, we got work to do!"

Dante and the warrior both saw the pirate and the monkey flee from the battlefield. They thought of them as cowards but Dante had no time to deal with them. He was focused on saving the other three Amazonians.

He attempted to use his sonic cannon blast on one of the Geode-mutants. It made contact with his foe but it merely got up ignoring the pain. So Dante switched tactics, he used his thrusters to get close to one of the creatures and then grabbed its arm. Then he began swinging the creature in circles before letting go and flinging his enemy at the other two Geode-mutants that were about to attack the Amazonian warriors.

Dante had successfully repelled the enemy attack from the prison grounds. The warrior who saw all this happen was grateful for what he had done. She was about to thank him but Dante's sensors were detecting something approaching.

Looking further out, more Geode-Mutants slowly entered the forest. Even the three that Dante took care of had gotten back up. The warrior couldn't believe what she was seeing. Dante braced himself for another battle but his systems were already warning him to not exert too much power, as he still hadn't fully recovered from his battle with Sarmaan.

Dante remained standing to protect the Amazonians and he refused to run away. He was about to be overwhelmed by the vast number of Geode-Mutants but a banana peel was thrown onto one of the creatures' heads and they all turned to the culprit. It was Sarmaan who threw the peel.

The monkey mocked the Geode-Mutants and their focus immediately shifted to him. Slowly they made their way towards the furball that insulted them, which was what Sarmaan wanted.

The Geode-Mutants followed Sarmaan away from the prison and into the forest where they lost sight of the monkey. They looked around but all they could see were trees in the surroundings and a rope beneath their feet. Liam pulled the rope from a tree he was sitting atop. The rope tightened and wrapped around all the mutants' legs.

"Alright Sarmaan, do it!"

Sarmaan transformed into his gorilla form and tackled all the Geode-Mutants that were tied together by the rope. They were knocked down into a deep pit that him and Liam had dug. At the top of the ditch, Liam laid down some blasting jelly to trigger a mudslide to collapse on the mutants. There was only one problem, Liam couldn't find a match.

The Geode-Mutants were beginning to untangle themselves out of their predicament. With enough time, they could escape the pit unless Liam could activate the blasting jelly. Liam looked everywhere around him but he could find nothing. Thankfully, Dante followed Sarmaan when he lured the Geode-Mutants. Using his cannon, he fired it at the blasting jelly, causing a chain reaction, collapsing the soil onto the creatures and burying them.

"Whew, that was a close one." As he wiped his forehead, Dante extended his hand to help him.

"Sorry, I thought you were a coward for running away." The cyborg apologized.

"Sarmaan and I have been on our own for a while. We have survived tougher battles than this."

Liam accepted Dante's help and as he pulled the pirate back up they both had a memory appear in their head. They somehow shared a memory where they were fighting together against a powerful foe. The location wasn't familiar but they could recognize each other's faces.

After the vision was over, they both said to each other simultaneously, "Wait, you are..." But their conversation would be interrupted as they heard a wailing sound echoing through the forest. It was coming from the Amazon tribe, where Myla was.

Queen of the Amazonians

While all the warriors were battling to keep the Borderlands protected, the queen was nowhere to be found on the frontline. Instead, she was wearing a cowl robe to hide herself away from everyone. She snuck into a secluded area where it was just her and a horse.

The horse was about to make a noise but the queen lowered her hood for a moment to calm her steed. When the horse settled, she was ready to hop on but before she could, she had a feeling someone was near. She pulled a sword that was kept by the harness of the horse and held it out to defend herself.

"Show yourself." Slowly a man stepped out of the shadow.

"Is that any way to treat someone you haven't seen in so long?" Rice replied.

"There's no way, you are still alive?"

"Well, I'm breathing and talking to you so I guess there is a way!" He jested.

"What do you want?"

"I don't want anything in particular. I'm just curious as to why the great Amazonian Queen would be running away instead of helping her people."

"Stop, that person is long gone."

"You are scared of him, aren't you?"

"Yes. How could you not be? You lost someone..." She couldn't complete the sentence as she saw the look on his face.

"I know, but we can't lose faith now. There is still hope."

"In what? Those students of yours?"

"They have grown. They aren't as dependent as you once remembered them to be."

The queen paused for a moment. "Even so, they are far too inexperienced. They won't stand a chance against him!"

"Not on their own, they will need guidance. Which is why I'm here to see you. Will you help them, Queen of the Amazonians?"

Back on the frontlines, the warriors were doing their best to hold against the Geode-Mutants. They were experiencing difficulty until Myla and Aria appeared on the scene. Aria pounded through the mutants with her gauntlets while Myla danced through her enemies and kicked them aside.

With their efforts, the Geode-Mutants were repelled back. The warriors lifted their weapons to celebrate their victory. Aria was so excited she was about to give Myla a massive hug but Myla didn't share their excitement. She felt something was wrong because the fight felt too easy.

It only took a moment to confirm her feelings. Echoing through the borderland was a terrifying wail that sent chills down everyone's spine. Myla knew this sound all too well as the source of the noise appeared out of the forest. It was the same creature that Myla saw from the Polluted Wilds.

While Myla was frozen in her thoughts, the group of warriors charged towards the beast that appeared. They let out a warcry and raised their weapons in unison to increase their morale, but the creature stood with confidence. It took in a deep breath and then let out a wail that blew away all its enemies.

Warriors were scattered through the area, heavily wounded. Seeing so many of her comrades injured, Aria bolted towards the beast. Myla saw Aria and she attempted to call her back. "Wait, stop! That thing is too strong!" But Aria never heard.

As Aria rushed up to the creature, she called for any warriors who were able to fight to aid her. Four other warriors rallied to her as they took on the enemy that injured many of their sisters in battle.

Aria jumped up and punched the enemy right on the forehead but the creature shook off the attack. She was shocked as to how tough the beast was but she continued to throw jabs to keep the creature's attention on her. While she was distracting the beast, the other warriors each had a rope that they threw at each of the beast's limbs.

With the creature's movement restricted, Aria stopped with her weak attacks. Instead, she charged up her dominant arm and was ready to run full force to finish the beast. Once she felt her focus was at its peak, she rushed toward the enemy, ready to deliver her strongest attack.

With Aria approaching, tears suddenly emerged from its eyes. It gushed out like a huge torrent and washed away the four warriors that were holding it down. Without any restraints, it swung its arms at Aria and connected with a brutal hit. Aria was sent flying and she slammed against one of the structures in the camp.

She was badly injured and unable to pick herself up while her enemy was slowly approaching her. It was about to reach out its hand to grab the wounded fighter but jumping to intercept was Myla. She swung a kick right at the creature's face but it had no effect.

Myla was so stunned by the result she couldn't react as the beast threw her aside. She immediately got back to her feet but she was too far to help Aria now. "No, Aria run!" But she was in too much pain. It reached out its arm again to grab its prey but out of nowhere, a dagger was thrown that impaled the arm of the monster.

The creature backed away from Aria, as it was holding its arm in pain. It attempted to pull out the dagger but its fingers couldn't reach the tiny weapon. As it was focused on trying to get rid of its agony, a woman appeared with a claymore and attacked the beast from multiple angles.

With its pain multiplying by the second, tears began to fill its eyes but before they could surge out, the woman struck the beast in the gut with all her might, forcing it to close its eyes. It then attempted to let out its deafening wail but again, the fighter had the beast figured out. She used her rope and wrapped it around the beast's mouth. Now the beast was silenced, and she finished off her enemy with one final swing of her sword.

After the creature collapsed to the ground, the woman made her way to Aria. Upon seeing the warrior who took down their foe, Aria quickly got to her knees as did all the other Amazonian warriors who witnessed the battle. It was the Queen of the Amazonians who had come to their rescue.

The queen didn't want further praise, asking everyone to get up and get their injuries treated immediately. She helped Aria up and together they made their way towards Myla.

She couldn't believe how strong the queen was. This whole time she had such a poor perception of her because of their first encounter. But after witnessing her tussle against the Geode-stone beast, Myla had new respect for the queen. While she was still on the ground, the queen reached out her hand to Myla. Immediately, Myla went on her knees and bowed.

"My apologies your Majesty. I was rude to your honour when I first arrived in your tribe. Despite my arrogance, you have saved my life and I am forever indebted to you."

"It is I who must ask for your apology. Despite how I treated you, you risked your life to help my comrades and defend our home. A task that you had no obligation to accept. For this, I must thank you."

The queen reached out an open hand to Myla. It was a sign that the queen was open to welcoming Myla into the Amazon Borderland as one of her own. Myla had a smile on her face, she reached for the queen's hand and got up on her feet. They were about to walk together to celebrate their new friendship but suddenly, something pierced through the queen's lower rib.

The preemptive attack had Myla, Aria, and all the Amazonian warriors looking on in horror. The queen suddenly grew weak and was about to collapse onto the ground. Thankfully, Aria and Myla caught her and rested her on the ground. They then looked up to see who was responsible.

What they found was another creature, one that Myla had also seen before in the Polluted Wilds. The one that launched shards of Geode-stones from its hair. Aria and Myla stared down their new adversary as it had only one thing to say in its raspy voice, "Doomeddddddd…"

Duo Diamond Strike

"Come on Liam, we got to move faster. Even Sarmaan is keeping up!"

"Hey! Easy for you two!" He was huffing a bit. "You are half machine and he's a monkey!"

"Sigh, I'm going on ahead, just do your best to catch up." Right as Dante was about to activate his rocket boost, Sarmaan popped onto his shoulder and hitched a ride.

"Sarmaan! You traitor!"

Thanks to the speed of the boosters, he made it to where the battle was happening much sooner. However, when he arrived, he found everyone in a dire situation. He could see all the Amazonian warriors scattered through the battlefield injured. Eventually, he found Myla standing alongside one of the warriors, which gave him relief. But his sensors would be on full alert as they detected the threat level of the monster that they were facing.

Dante could see from afar that the creature was ready to unleash a big attack. He had his computer calculate what its target would be and when he received the information, he immediately went down to assist Myla and Aria.

On the battlefield, the creature had the hair on its head all raised. Myla and Aria could see the hair crystallizing and they were bracing themselves for the attack. The monster shot the crystals in the air and it was about to rain down from the sky. When Myla and Aria could see the shards falling, they realized they weren't the targets. The creature was aiming for all the injured warriors.

Myla and Aria looked at each other hoping either would have a plan. Unfortunately, there was no time or option for them. They looked on into the sky where they noticed something opposing the rain of crystals.

Dante used his rocket booster to take him to the skies. This got him closer to the crystals where they were still clustered together. He channelled all power to create a defensive shield that would block all the incoming Geode-stones. Dante held the forcefield up for as long as he could but some of the crystals got through and struck him.

The good news was none of the crystals harmed anyone else. But because some of the shards struck Dante, it shut off parts of his system and he dropped to the ground. He landed hard on impact but when Myla rushed up to him, he held a thumbs up to signify that he would be alright.

Myla felt reassured knowing Dante was okay but when she turned to look at her opponent her eyes changed to ones of anger. She turned to Aria and told her their new plan of attack.

"What! You are crazy!" Aria yelled.

"Conventional tactics won't cut it against this opponent. We have to try it." Myla stood her ground on the idea and eventually Aria gave in to her conviction.

Starting off, Aria ran around to the creature's blind side. The creature rotated its head and could sense Aria so it fired two shards from its hair. Aria deflected them away with her gauntlets which allowed Myla to engage the enemy.

Seeing Myla running directly at it, the monster fired again. Myla used her nimbleness and avoided as many of the shards as possible. A second barrage of Geode-stones was unleashed, so what Myla couldn't avoid, Aria jumped in and blocked everything with her gauntlets.

The pressure was now on the creature, seeing Myla closing the gap. It felt as if it had no choice but to overpower her. Again, it directed the shards right at Myla but Aria began punching the ground and using the rocks that came from it as a shield against the projectiles.

Now, Myla was in point-blank range, and she unleashed the hardest roundhouse right at the jaw of the creature. It pushed back the creature a bit but was ready to strike back. It looked as if Myla's plan had failed but in actuality, that was not the case.

"Alright Aria, she's all yours!"

With Myla in such proximity, the creature's vision was blocked and it had forgotten about Aria. She had a Geode-stone and she placed it into her crystal gauntlet. Aria launched herself at full speed and landed a right cross with her gauntlet overflowing with Geode-stone energy.

After the hit landed, both Myla and Aria had a strange yet familiar feeling. Their ability to work together so well wasn't very common among most people. They suddenly had a small memory when they sparred together but from when they were unclear. However, one thing they were sure of, they had met before.

"Aria, you and I were..."

Before Myla could finish, Aria lunged towards her and pushed her aside. As she was falling, she could see a crystal spike piercing Aria in the right shoulder. Aria fell on one knee as the Geode-stone hair monster reappeared after surviving a devastating blow.

Slowly joining everyone else was Liam who had finally made his way. "Oh boy, that was a lot of running. Finally, I can get some..." He looked up and he saw the damage that had already been done.

"Uh oh, Myla is in trouble! What am I going to do?!" He was in a state of panic but he felt someone pulling him. "Sarmaan! You are alive! What are we going to do?!" Sarmaan points in a direction and Liam looks over to see Dante lying down and unable to move, so he rushes over to him.

"Dante! What happened to you? You are in terrible shape."

"I might be in much better shape if someone didn't take his sweet time."

"Hey! Are you calling me slow?"

"We have no time for this. Do you still have the bag you stole from me?"

"Uh, maybe... I can't confirm or deny that information."

"Please tell me you have it. This is very important."

Liam was a bit embarrassed but he pulled out the bag and showed it to Dante. "There's a stone in there, give it to Myla."

He reached his hands in and when he pulled out the stone. "What?! This is a Geode-stone! How did you get this?!"

"There's no time! Give it to Myla!" He grabbed the Geode-stone immediately and was on his way.

Myla was about to help Aria but the creature launched her spikes and created a small enclosure preventing her from escaping. Myla could only watch as Aria was about to be defeated by the enemy.

"MYLA!" There was a loud voice that called for her name. Myla looked and rolling down a hill to get to her was Liam who had a special delivery for her. She accepted what Liam had given her and upon contact with the Geode-stone, she felt a huge influx of energy.

The creature was ready to land the final strike but it felt a tap on its shoulder that it could not ignore. Turning around it was met with a kick to the face, that sent it a few meters back. Myla then held her hand out to Aria who noticed that her energy level was different.

"You got enough for one more round?" Myla asked.

"You bet I do."

Aria got up and she looked reenergized despite the wound on her shoulder. Both of the fighters stood back to back and then engaged against their enemy with focus and determination.

The crystal beast was hiding its fear as it could sense something had changed between the two fighters. It attempted to disrupt their rhythm by launching its Geode-stone spikes but all its attacks were either evaded or deflected away as Myla and Aria moved fully synchronized to close the gap.

Once they were in range, the elite Geode-Mutant froze in fear. Aria raised her dominant fist into the air while Myla got ready to unleash her whirlwind kick. A abundant amount of energy was gathered between the two and with the power flowing in them they looked at each other as they had this feeling before.

"You still remember how this goes?" Myla asked with a smile.

"Ha, as if I would ever forget!"

They jumped into the air and the energy from the Geode-stones combined. The sheer aura was felt by the beast as all its muscles could no longer move. In unison, they attacked together and called out their special technique. "Duo Diamond Strike!"

Atonement

Myla and Aria connected with their attack, causing a massive impact that could be felt standing miles away. Everyone waited for the smoke to clear and as it did, they could see their enemy was unable to move.

Liam and Sarmaan began jumping for joy as they did a happy dance. "THEY DID IT! THEY DID IT! WOOOOOOO!"

"Well done..." Dante was still low on power but he had enough to witness the great feat the two fighters accomplished.

Myla and Aria were exhausted after what they had just done. All they wanted to do was just lie down for a moment and not move. As they both lay down on their backs, they had a huge laugh and memories of their past were coming back to them.

"We were friends before!" Myla initiated.

"Yeah! We met at a school or something." Aria replied.

"But why couldn't we remember any of it up until now?"

"I don't know but I hope we never forget again."

The two friends were glad to be reunited. However, their moment would be cut short as they both felt another unsettling aura. There was an unexpected draft that brushed through them and appearing on the other side of the battlefield was a creature that Myla had never seen before.

This one was smaller than the other two but its speed was in a class of its own. No one could see its movement as it ran past them and made its way to the other defeated Geode-stone monsters. Myla managed to catch a glimpse of its movement and she realized it looked very familiar.

"That thing, it moves like..."

Before she could finish, a mass of Geode-Mutants appeared. They rallied around the two fallen beasts that were defeated and carried them away. The speedy enemy remained for a moment to stared at Myla, before fleeing into the forest.

The Borderlands were safe again but it came at a heavy cost. Many of the Amazon warriors were heavily injured, along with the queen who was lying down in what appeared to be her final moments. A few of the warriors gathered around her but she wasn't ready to depart yet as she asked to speak with both Myla and Aria.

The two were brought near the queen. She asked if they could get closer so she didn't have to raise her voice.

"Myla, Aria, I'm sorry."

"You don't have to say anything, your honour! You risked your life to save us! Now please, save your breath!" Aria pleaded.

"No, I have much to tell you both. Aria, you weren't always an Amazonian."

"Wait what?" She had the look of shock on her.

"You always had the strength and heart of one, but you weren't born in the borderlands. That is why you never felt like you fit in and why you were drawn to Myla."

"If I'm not from here then where am I from?"

"The upper city."

"Upper city? Zenith?!" Aria asked and the queen confirmed.

"About two years ago, there was a man who brought you here while you were unconscious. He told me to keep you here and raise you as if you have lived in the borderlands your entire life. I had no idea what his intentions were but he threatened to destroy the entire borderlands and my people if I didn't comply. I tried to rebel against his offer but I was no match for him. Full of fear, I accepted his terms but little did I know I became a slave that day. If I ever rejected any of his commands, he would threaten to turn back on his word and harm my people. I have done many horrible things that I cannot take back. I'm not deserving to be called your queen."

Aria still had much to take in but she held the hand of the queen. "You did what you thought was best and you did it to protect your people. I'm honoured to call you my queen."

The queen smiled and shed some tears. However, she quickly turned to face Myla as she was not done.

"Myla, I can't thank you enough."

"It's nothing, you would do the same..."

"No. You not only helped save my people, but you also saved me."

"I don't understand..."

"The past few years have been the worst of my life. I was a coward and turned away from what a queen should stand against. But your arrival and actions are a huge reason why I was able to atone for my sins today. I now see why that man fears you..."

"That man? You mean the one who put Aria here?!"

"Yes, he is extremely dangerous and malevolent, and you need to stop him before it gets any worse."

"Where is he? Tell me who he is so Aria and I can beat the living snot out of him!"

"He's up in Zenith. He is ..." The pain in her wounds were intensifying, forcing her to cough profusely.

"Your honour! Stop talking! You have said enough, just rest!" Aria tried to get her to stop but the queen refused.

"Go to Zenith. I have a feeling everything will be made clear there."

The grip on her hand was loosening from Aria's hand but she had enough strength to relay one last message to the remaining warriors who were standing. "My sisters in arms, it has been an honour for me to serve as your queen. I hope my final actions can serve as an atonement for the pain I have caused you all." Those were her final words and her eyes closed.

The rain poured down as Aria slammed her fist in agony. Liam, Sarmaan, and Dante looked on and remained silent during such a solemn time. All the other warriors kneeled on the ground to pay respect to their queen. And then there was Myla, who looked towards the direction they needed to go.

"Zenith, here we come."

The Captain

After narrowly escaping the enforcers and bloodhounds, Max, Netanya, and Ajay needed a place to hide. Because Max was an enforcer, he had information about the layout of Zenith including which buildings were abandoned or occupied. He found one that was clear for them to take cover in.

Ajay could hear noises through his ears but they weren't clear enough for him to identify whose they were. His consciousness was slowly coming back after being badly injured. His vision was initially blurry but it was slowly coming to focus.

"He's waking up! Ajay, you are awake!" Netanya announced.

"Ugh, what happened? Feels like I got hit by Doctor Ashima's hammer." Ajay said while putting pressure on his head.

"It wasn't that, but you were beaten up pretty bad. Luckily, he came to help you!" Netanya pointed to Max.

"Hi." He introduced himself with a monotone voice.

"Uh hi? Do I know you? Ajay sounded confused.

"You do! I mean you did..."

"Huh? I don't get what you're saying." Ajay was still confused so Netanya flipped to a page in one of her books.

"Here Ajay, take a look at this picture." It was a class photo that had both Max and Ajay in it. After Ajay had some time with the photo, Netanya pointed to where his focus should be next, the year the photo was taken.

"We were in the same class two years ago? But I don't remember him at all..."

"Ajay I know it might sound crazy, but I think somehow we have forgotten what happened two years ago."

Ajay was at a loss for words. His head was still hurting from the injuries he sustained. Then Max decided to break his silence and share his experience.

"I think Netanya is correct. While I was sent to Nadir, I ran into someone and started to have flashbacks. I can't remember them all and most of it doesn't make sense. However, I keep having the strange feeling that I should have known who she was."

"Is she in this picture?" Netanya asked while holding the book to Max and he pointed to the person.

"Her? She's..."

Both Netanya and Ajay were starting to have a headache but their memories would be cut short as someone appeared before them with an unwelcoming presence. Standing behind them was a person in an enforcer uniform and mask. However, this enforcer was distinguished with an 'S' emblem on his uniform.

"Well well. So you finally showed your true colours, private Max." The voice sounded lower-toned as it was filtered through the mask.

Max pulled out his stun baton to prepare for battle. He knew Ajay was in no condition to fight and getting Netanya involved wouldn't be in their best interest. In such a situation, he told Netanya to grab Ajay and leave but both Ajay and Netanya disagreed with his choice.

"Don't worry, I don't intend on having any of you leave here today." The captain drew out his weapon. It was a long staff that had electricity pulsing from both ends.

Max ran straight at the captain and his weapon clashed with his enemy's, putting them in a deadlock. "Leave now!" He yelled at the former students. Despite not liking the situation, Netanya began pulling Ajay who could only hobble at best. The captain could see them moving towards the exit but he was determined not to let them escape.

First, he applied more force and pushed Max against the wall. That freed his electrical staff, allowing him to aim two electrical discharges at both the runaway fugitives. He landed a hit on both their backs, stunning them.

With both his targets immobilized, he was ready to approach them but grabbing him from behind was Max. The captain swung around frantically to get him to let go.

"What are you doing? Don't you realize the Headmaster is just using you?"

As Max tried to persuade the captain to listen, he slammed Max against the building wall. Max was forced to let go and as he was lying on the ground, the captain grabbed his staff and shocked Max to paralyze him.

"I don't listen to traitors."

He had all three targets dealt with and he was ready to call in reinforcement to help carry them away. However, before he could contact anyone, he felt a fire arrow behind him, which he barely evaded.

"That attack, it could only be..." When he looked at the direction it came from he saw four people who he thought he had previously disposed of. Willyham, Devan, Arnav, and Harshitha were standing there.

"How is it possible that you are all still alive?" The captain asked in outrage.

"Yes captain, please tell me, how are they still alive?" There was a reply but it was one that none of them were expecting. The very voice sent chills down everyone's spine and had them all paralyzed in fear.

"Headmaster Volice! I didn't know, I thought they were trapped in the explosion!" The captain panicked as he tried to plead his case.

"Sigh, how disappointing. I want to overlook this failure, but it is as you said captain, I don't listen to traitors."

Voiice grew suspicious of the captain's activity and without even moving, the headmaster knocked out the captain in an instant.

After witnessing what had happened, Harshitha told Willyham to see if he could help Netanya, Ajay, and the other enforcer on the ground. Willyham listened, leaving Harshitha, Arnav, and Devan to face the Headmaster together.

Willyham quickly ran to Netanya and Ajay first. He shocked them hoping they would be able to get up but they were still paralyzed. However, Netanya could still speak, so she told Willyham to grab her crystal wand and use it to break their paralysis. Willyham found the wand lying near Netanya and he pointed it at them. Netanya gave him clear instructions on how to hold it and what to say.

Willyham waved the wand in the motion he was told and the wand cast a magical wave that fell over Netanya and Ajay. The magic also had a pretty bad recoil that sent Willyham falling on his bottom but he successfully rid Netanya and Ajay of their bind.

"Great job Willyham, now take the wand and go use it on the enforcer right there!"

"Wait what? I thought they were the bad guys!"

"That one is good! Just trust me!"

So Willyham picked up the crystal wand and made his way to Max. Meanwhile, Netanya rushed to where the captain was lying down. She couldn't explain it but she had a bad feeling in her gut. Carefully, she took off the mask and turned to the book that had the photo in it. She looked at every face in the photo and unfortunately, there was one that matched the captain's.

"Oh no... Saivik..."

Rendezvous

Harshitha and Arnav stood armed with their crystal weapons. Two highly ranked students were about to face their biggest test: a confrontation against the Headmaster of their school. They both took a deep breath before engaging in the fight of their lives.

Arnav took the lead placing his shield in front and charging forward but after taking just one step, his whole body froze.

"What's wrong Arnav? Weren't you going to attack me with your sword?" The Headmaster taunted.

With all his strength, Arnav tried to move his body but it would not work. Within a second, the Headmaster appeared in front of him, ready to strike him down. However, Harshitha cast an icy gust that forced the Headmaster to distance himself from Arnav.

"Ahh Harshitha, one of the highest-ranking students in Diamondvale. Try that again, I promise not to move." He stood still with his hands up, provoking Harshitha to cast her magic.

She had a feeling it was a trap but she couldn't resist such an opportunity. Using both her hands she attempted to cast a fire torrent spell but for some reason, she stopped midway. Like Arnav, her body would not respond to her commands.

With both the students immobilized, the Headmastered appeared behind Arnav and struck him behind. He then followed up by striking Harshitha in the back. In mere seconds, Headmaster Volice took down two high-ranking students of Diamondvale.

"How disappointing. An emerald and diamond ranked student, and neither could even lay a finger on me. No point in delaying the inevitable, I'll finish you both right ..."

He was interrupted by Devan, who charged in and attempted to tackle him. The Headmaster was able to evade the first tackle along with the second follow-up.

"So you finally decide to join the battle, Devan. I thought you would be too scared after what happened at the coliseum."

Again, he was provoking his enemy and it worked, Devan went straight for Volice but unlike Arnav and Harshitha who were unsuccessful, Devan broke through. But even though Devan couldn't be frozen by Volice, the Headmaster could still avoid his attacks.

"Not bad. It seems 'he' has taught you how to get around some of my techniques."

"Quit talking old man! I'm going to take you down!" Devan was filled with anger.

Devan went of another tackle and that was when the tide of the battle shifted. In one instance, Volice reached out his arm and grabbed Devan in the face. He then threw him back against the ground, causing Devan to slide to where Arnav and Harshitha were lying down.

With Arnav, Harshitha, and Devan unable to get up, Volice moved towards them. However, impeding his way were Willyham and Ajay who had stepped in. They were both extremely nervous but they refused to run.

"I will give you two a C for courage. But an F for foolish!" Without warning he winded both Ajay and Willyham and they both fell to the ground.

Now there was only one person who was left standing, Netanya who reclaimed her wand and stood before the Headmaster.

"Netanya, you always struck me as a reasonable person. Are you seriously going to fight me all by yourself?"

"I'm not going to fight you."

"Very smart, then stand aside!"

"I will but before I do, I have one thing to ask."

"Stalling for time, a cunning tactic. Alright, I'll answer one question."

"Where is Vihaan?"

"Oh, so you remember about Doctor Vihaan? It appears you do know too much..."

"All I know is that you forced him to do your vile experiments," Netanya replied.

"Forced? I did no such thing. I merely, let's say, persuaded him."

"What you are doing is wrong! Those experiments are inhumane!"

"Silence!"

He had a burst of anger and his aura was so oppressing it forced Netanya to become silent. "I have lived many times your age. Don't think you can judge what is humane based on your limited knowledge. Now you will pay for your foolish words."

The aura was growing stronger and Netanya couldn't handle it any longer. The pressure was becoming unbearable and she was nearly out of air but a sonic blast forced the Headmaster to jump out of the way and disrupt his focus.

Netanya had been saved by Dante's heroics and he wasn't the only one there. Standing behind him were Liam with Sarmaan on his shoulder, Aria, and Myla.

Devan saw Dante as he was still lying on his belly. "Well, it's about bloody time you showed up."

"Sorry to keep you waiting, but I got everyone here now," Dante replied.

The Headmaster was severely annoyed by all the interruptions. Again he unleashed his oppressing aura and caught Liam, Sarmaan, Aria, and Myla. Seeing that they were so easily trapped by his power, he saw them as no threat. However, Dante interrupted him again with another pulse blast from his arm.

"Ahh, Dante, the machine. It appears you have been trained by 'him' as well. No matter."

Volice appeared behind Dante and stabbed a Geode-stone in his back. The crystal was strong enough to pierce through the robotic plating and it was short-circuiting his body. His entire system was warning him of a malfunction as he was losing power to his entire body.

With Dante no longer able to move, the Headmaster turned his attention back to the other four warriors he had paralyzed in his aura. "Let's see who are these people you have brought with you, Dante."

He first saw Liam and Sarmaan. "Ahh the pirate and his sidekick monkey."

Sarmaan was not happy with his comment and he began flailing his arms and legs in objection. "Yeah! Whatever Sarmaan is saying, I second that!" Liam added on.

Volice tossed them aside and then moved on to the next. "Aria, the girl who I asked the Queen of the Amazonian to take in. Seems you somehow managed to survive in that environment and have become even stronger."

Aria tried to use all the strength in her body to punch the man but his power was too oppressive. "But not strong enough." Similar to what he did to Liam and Sarmaan, he also used his power to push Aria and slam her against the ground. He now moved on to the last person.

"And you must be Myla. The one whom the Queen of the Amazonians told me was on her way."

"You... YOU ARE THE ONE WHO BLACKMAILED THE QUEEN! I WILL...!" She tried to kick him but Volice wouldn't allow it.

He looked to have complete control of the situation but he didn't realize Aria was still conscious when Myla was speaking. Hearing what Myla said, Aria had a huge spike of energy and she shot out with haste, appearing near the Headmaster.

Volice was caught off guard but he managed to dodge Aria's right cross punch. He was about to counter but Myla threw a low kick that the Headmaster barely dodged.

For a moment, Voice showed a sign of sweat dripping from his forehead. That led Aria and Myla to believe that had a chance against their opponent but he quickly dashed their hopes when he slammed his fist on the ground. The motion created a heavy force of gravity that pinned them down.

"Enough foolish games. I will end it here, once and for all."

He was about to channel a massive amount of energy to obliterate all the fighters who stood against him but someone's presence caught Voice's attention. He recognized who it was without even looking.

"Finally decided to show up, Professor Rice?" The man did not respond. "Tch, it doesn't matter, you can't save them."

Voice was about to raise his hand and everyone who was defeated began bracing themselves for his attack. However, Rice instantly appeared before him and grabbed his wrist, preventing the Headmaster from harming anyone. Everyone including Voice was shocked, as they didn't think anyone was capable of stopping the headmaster's attack.

Voice shook his hand free and distanced himself from his opponent. He checked his hand and although it didn't suffer significant damage, he had wasted much energy in his other battles. He decided to retreat but not without saying a few more words. "Heh, looks like you were able to rescue the ones here, but there are some you still haven't been able to save."

"Don't worry, we'll find you and we will save them all."

"Haha, good luck. I will be waiting." With that, the Headmaster disappeared.

The fighters that stood up against Headmaster Voice had avoided devastation thanks to the man known as Rice. However, many of them were confused as to who this man was and how he was connected to them. It was Devan and Dante who let everyone know that Rice was on their side and he was once their teacher.

The Professor

T*wo years ago...*
Inside the school of Diamondvale, a class of twenty-two students were waiting in the training grounds room for their teacher to arrive. They were all excited about the self-defence class that appeared only once on their weekly schedule. It was going to be taught by their new teacher, Professor Rice. While most of them were able to contain their enthusiasm, there were a few who had other ideas.

"Guys, I found one of these lying outside of the training equipment room!" Yelled Devan holding a ball with spikes.

"Hey don't hog it! Pass it over!" Sahil rushed over to try and take it but Sarmaan stole it from Devan's hands.

"Ha! Good luck getting this now. I'm the tallest one here so there's no way any of you can reach..." He then gets tackled by Liam. "Hey! What are you doing?"

"I GOT HIM PINNED GUYS! GET IT!" Liam yelled.

Aria and Myla decided to look away and pretend not to know them.

"I don't think you guys should be doing this. I think the professor will show up soon." Netanya kindly advised them.

"Yeah yeah, whatever No-Fun-Netanya. Quit being a party pooper!" Saivik threw the insult without thinking. His words put Netanya in a sorrowful mood.

Myla saw what happened and couldn't stand for it. She was ready to run up to the boys and give them a beating of a lifetime and Aria was there to join her. They had their fists ready but Arnav and Dante jumped in in hopes of calming them down. Their words weren't very effective so they asked for Harshitha to help them but she was ignoring everyone and reading her book.

So Aria and Myla pushed the two boys aside and went straight at the five hooligans. With Liam, Sarmaan, Saivik, Sahil and Devan already in a pile fighting for the ball, Myla and Aria jumped in as well. They were locked in a huge mess and there was so much chaos the ball rolled out into the open.

Ajay saw the spike ball all by itself and he heard it calling to him. He kicked it so hard it first went in Leo's direction but just barely missed him. It continued on and then hit Dylan square in the face.

Max knew what was about to happen. He rushed over in hopes of preventing the waterworks but it was too late. Dylan's eyes immediately had tears gushing out and with his mouth wide open he let out a wail that could be heard through the room.

"Tell him to stop!" Yelled an aggravated Jacob.

"Don't worry everyone, I think I can help him!" Ashima suggested but everyone advised against it.

Suddenly Dylan stopped his wailing. Everyone was relieved and they could let go and hear again but they wouldn't be relaxed for long. They all shifted their attention to the entrance of the training room where their teacher was standing with his arms crossed.

"Uh oh... We are doomed..." Sissi said in a quiet voice.

"Everyone against the wall now." His voice wasn't loud but his tone was serious.

Within seconds, everyone was lined up with their backs against the wall. They watched as he held the spike ball in one hand.

"Alright class is now in session. Your first challenge, try not to get hit by an object I throw for one whole minute. You are free to run anywhere in this room, those are the rules. If you survive, nothing will happen! But if you fail, well I'll just tell you later!" He said this all with a smile on his face.

The entire class was confused. They thought they would be handed a tougher punishment but the task the professor threw out didn't seem too hard. Maybe Professor Rice wasn't as difficult as they initially thought.

"Are you all ready?" They all nodded their heads and he returned a smile.

He then threw the ball in the opposite direction which had everyone in the room perplexed. The object was going nowhere near them but they were so focused on the spike ball, that the professor pulled out a bunch of random objects he had hidden. He began throwing them all at them and he tagged every single one of them before the time limit expired.

"Well, it looks like you were unable to complete my challenge, what an unfortunate turn of events."

"Hey, that's not fair! You cheated! We thought we only had to dodge the spike ball!" Yelled Ashima.

"First rule of self-defence, there are no rules." He replied without hesitation.

"Come on professor, I think you are exaggerating a bit..."

Devan broke off in his sentence as Rice had somehow disappeared and reappeared behind him. Everyone else in the class was paralyzed in fear too as he did that without anyone seeing him move a muscle.

"Against a real enemy, they won't play by any rules." As he said that, he moved his hands towards Devan's direction. Everyone thought Devan was about to get punched in the face. Devan shut his eyes but Rice had him fooled as all he did was flick Devan in between the eyes.

"Ow!"

"Okay lesson is over, but no one is allowed to leave until you all give me 50 laps around this room and 100 push-ups!"

There was a huge wave of complaints but he ran out of the room and before they could catch him. He was about to head out but meeting him outside the room was the Headmaster.

"You didn't have to be so hard on them for their first class."

"They will be fine. Besides, I learned these training tactics from you."

"Haha, you were a difficult one to get through, let's just say that."

"So what do you want? I know you don't just visit to give pleasantries."

"How very perceptive, I can't hide anything from you. As you know I'm doing research on the Geode-stones and I believe I'm about to reach a breakthrough."

"Go on..."

"There are a few students in your class that I would like to assist me in my research. I need all teachers to accept this proposal and you are the last one."

"Wow, putting all the pressure on me? In that case, you should have saved your time by asking me first. Because my answer is, no."

The answer caught Volice off-guard. "Professor Rice, please reconsider your decision! This research has the potential to increase people's lifespan and better yet, cure lethal diseases."

"You can find other volunteers, my students are off-limits. Have a nice day Headmaster."

He turned his back on Volice and walked away. The Headmaster was enraged by the professor's decision. He tried to get what he wanted the diplomatic way but now he had to resort to other tactics.

━━━━✕╫╲╲╲╋╲✕━━━━

One week later...

The professor was making his way to the self-defense class and he was going to be behind schedule again. He opened the entrance door, expecting chaos like his first encounter with the class but when the door opened, it was silent. At first, he thought a miracle had occurred but then he looked at the class carefully. A few of them were missing.

It was more than just a quiet environment, Rice felt the morale was low. "Hey, what's going on around here? I know I was tough on you for your first class but that's no reason to become disheartened!"

Most of the class stayed quiet but Ashima had enough energy to speak. "Dylan, Leo, Sarmaan, Vihaan and Saivik have been missing for a week and no one knows where they are."

Rice didn't respond. He had a feeling he knew what happened to them and he was thinking about his next course of action.

"We tried asking everyone around the school if they had seen them but the way they responded was so weird. It was as if they had no idea who they were or they never went to the school!" Willyham yelled.

After hearing what Willyham had to say, the professor stood up straight and his posture demanded their attention. "Everyone, today your class is going to be cancelled!" The entire class was dumbfounded by his answer.

"I just realized I was cooking something and I left the stove on. I got to get back before I set everything on fire! Goodbye!" And he booked it out of the room, leaving the students all by themselves.

"Well, that was weird." Commented Aria.

"Yeah, you would think he would be more responsible than to leave a stove on. That's not setting a very good example for us." Amrita chimed in.

"No Amrita, not that! Don't you think it's weird that he just dashed out randomly like that?"

"He knows something and he wasn't willing to tell us. We should follow him." Myla suggested.

Her suggestion was met with mixed decisions, about half the class thought it would be a great course of action. The other half elected to return to their dorms. The ones that stayed in the room with Myla were: Aria, Dante, Liam, Devan, Jacob, Sahil, Amrita, and Sissi.

"Alright everyone, let's go follow Professor Rice!" Myla yelled with confidence.

"So which way did he go?" Sahil asked.

"Oh I have no idea," Myla responded in defeat.

"Way to get our hopes up Myla! We don't even know where to start!" Jacob exclaimed.

"Oh no, we're doomed..." Sissi added on.

"Hey, all of you stop blaming Myla! I don't see any of you coming up with better ideas!" Aria stood up for Myla and everyone became quiet knowing she had a point. They all apologized for their poor attitude towards her.

"It's alright everyone, you are all just worried about them, I am too, and we will figure out a way to find them." She affirmed.

"HEY GUYS!" Dante yelled and everyone turned to him. "Finally! I have been trying to get your attention for the past five minutes!"

"Our bad, I guess we were too focused on giving Myla a difficult time," Liam replied.

"HEY!" Myla shouted.

"Okay stop it, everyone. I know where Professor Rice is headed."

"What?! How in the world did you manage to figure that out?" Devan asked in amazement.

Dante pulled out a device that showed a grid on a screen with a dot flashing. It was a tracking device and Dante had managed to put a tracking chip on Rice before he left the room. Although everyone was happy he had the solution to their problem, they were skeptical as to how he had a tracking device.

"You should all have one. Our technology professor taught us how to make one in class!"

They all looked at him with blank stares and that was when Dante realized, no one except for him paid attention to the professor in that class. But it was a good thing Dante listened, otherwise, they would not have been able to locate where Professor Rice had run off to. So they all allowed Dante to lead the way.

Experiments

The following are accounts from a logbook written by Doctor Vihaan three years ago. This was one of the books Netanya 'borrowed' from the library.

This is Doctor Vihaan writing here. I have been assigned to be the lead scientist for this project which Headmaster Volice has been very excited about. He wasn't too clear on the specifics but he talked about the potential of healing the sick and improving health for all of humanity. I wanted to be part of this great vision so I humbly agreed to help him.

Day 1

On the first day working in this lab, I was given many Geode-stones to research. In their solid state, it was very difficult to test them so they had to be broken down and turned into liquid form. The process was long and tedious but I managed to get them done in a reasonable amount of time. What I found from these Geode-stones were properties, unlike anything I had witnessed before. They contained many mysterious substances that I would need to further investigate. Headmaster Volice assured me that he would provide the perfect test subjects so I just need to focus on my work.

Day 5

It's been a few days since I first started working on this project for Headmaster Volice. The Geode-stones were far more technologically complex than I expected. It's been very difficult to find ways to combine and synthesize compounds that would work with them. I have lost count of how many trials failed but I finally came up with a couple of concoctions that might succeed. Headmaster Volice said there were a couple of volunteers who were willing to test the concoctions.

Day 6

The test subjects have taken the compound and are experiencing some positive results! Subject A was given the first compound which was a mix of Geode-stone dust and monkey genetics. The mixture has given him an increase in his speed, energy and even the ability to climb!

Moving on to Subject L, he seems to be a small yet jolly soul. We gave him the second infusion that contained the Geode-stone dust and lion genetics. It's only been the first day but the subject has seemed to have increased in determination and bravery.

Both subjects have shown incredibly positive results and I told the Headmaster that we would continue to monitor their progress but he insisted that we move on to the next experiment. That was when he introduced the third test subject, Subject D. He wanted me to commence with the project and that he would return in about a week for the results. He even assigned a security guard to make sure no one came to harm me or the experiments. He wore a mask on at all times so I never got to see his face. We never really spoke and the only thing I remember about him was that he had a S-emblem on his uniform.

Day 8

I have continued to monitor the progress of Subject A and Subject L. Their animal instincts seemed to have gotten stronger with each passing day but they maintained their human figure. However, there was a glaring side effect from the Geode-stone compound that I could not ignore, it caused memory loss. It was here that I began to have doubts about what I was doing. I wasn't sure if Headmaster Volice was honest when he said this research would improve the living conditions of humanity. Because of that, I never commenced with the experiment of Subject D.

Day 11

Today was the day I saw the full extent of the side effects of the experiments. Subject A and Subject L were no longer human. Instead, Subject A had transformed into a monkey while Subject L became a Lion. Full of rage, they rattled their cage with Subject L successfully breaking down his prison looking to attack me. My life nearly flashed before my eyes but thankfully, the security guard that Volice assigned saved me.

After pushing me out of the way, he was pinned to the ground by the lion. I was scared but I knew I couldn't just run or stand there and watch helplessly. I immediately pulled myself together and managed to find the sedation in the lab and inject it into the lion before it could cause further harm. The guard placed the lion back into its cage and then turned back to his station. We never spoke a word to each other before and we still didn't that day.

✝✝⎥⎥✝✝

D*ay 13*
   Headmaster Volice returned to the lab today and I told him I would not continue with the research project. He would not accept no for an answer. He showed me a photo of a young boy. He told me my research could potentially save the boy's life.

His tone felt sincere and when he looked me directly in the eyes, I couldn't feel any lies. From there I decided to begin the experiment on subject D. As I was preparing the compound, I had one question that had been going through my head. I asked Volice who the boy in the photograph was but before he could answer, a man appeared in the lab that I had never seen before.

I attempted to eavesdrop on their conversation. It appeared the man was named Professor Rice and he demanded for Volice to release his students. The headmaster insisted he had no idea what the professor was saying and the events escalated into a battle. I never witnessed the fight as their power clash sent me into a different room.

When I picked myself up I noticed a group of students that appeared in my lab. They were working together to break Subjects A and L free. As I held out my hand telling them to stop, they turned around and called me by my name. I was confused as to how they knew me when I had never met them. They kept trying to convince me that I was their classmate but I had no memories of how these people related to me.

Our conversation would be cut short as the entire laboratory was beginning to shake. The battle between the headmaster and the professor was causing the entire place to become unstable. There was debris falling from the ceiling and some of it fell into the gas chamber, causing a combustion that was heading my way. Many of them yelled out for me to move out of the way but my legs were frozen. I would have sustained catastrophic injuries but instead, I was saved by one of them, I believe his name was Dante.

However, because of his effort, he lost a majority of his limbs and was in critical condition. His friends were in distress and although I didn't recognize him, something in my heart told me to help him. I did my best to utilize the equipment in the room to stabilize his condition. I found some mechanical augmentations lying around in the room that I attached to replace his limbs. It was a miracle this man survived.

After healing Dante, Professor Rice was smashed through a wall and landed in the same room as everyone. He was slow to get up as it seemed like he was losing the fight against the Headmaster. As he got up, he saw the condition of Dante and all the students who had followed him without him knowing. His major concern was no longer stopping Volice but his student's safety.

The professor carried Dante and told them that they had to escape immediately. However, one of them didn't listen. He shouted that he wasn't going to leave until he found Sarmaan. He separated from the pack and that's when the Headmaster appeared. Professor Rice attempted to attack Volice to give everyone a chance to escape, but more debris fell from the ceiling. The professor, Dante, and Devan got separated from the group.

The remaining group of students were left to fight against the Headmaster. Sahil, Jacob, Amrita, Sissi and Aria all charged at him simultaneously but they were casted aside. However, their attack was just a diversion, giving way for Myla to land a kick on the Headmaster's blindside. She came the closest of any of the students to harming Volice but he still managed to grab her by the throat. Seeing her as a potential threat, he was ready to end it right there but Aria jumped in between to intervene.

She managed to get Volice to release Myla from her grasp but now Aria was about to suffer the Headmaster's wrath. But another explosion erupted from the lab, which created a massive dust cloud from the powdered Geode-stones that spread through the entire lab.

Day 14

I woke up the next day after the explosion and found the damage it had caused. Subject A and L were both missing along with the professor and nearly all the students as well. The only one that remained was the one called Aria who was unconscious. Headmaster Volice was about to take out his anger on her after all the progress lost in the experiment. However, I stepped in and told the headmaster not to harm Aria.

He wouldn't listen to me until I told him that I promised to start the experiment on subject D if he would let Aria go.

He agreed and over the next week, he would gather the resources needed to repair the lab to get it functioning again. In addition, he left Aria in the care of the Amazonian tribe.

Day 20

As I was waiting for the lab to finish with the repairs, I wandered into the wilds by myself as I grew lonely. Thankfully, it was on this day that I found a new companion. It was a lizard but it had Geode-stones coming out from its back. My hunch was that the exposure to all the Geode-stone waste caused it to mutate into what it is now. I felt bad for the poor creature and decided to take care of it.

Day 104

It took three months for the lab to be repaired and operational. Once the building opened up again, I returned to work with the lizard creature by my side. Unfortunately, Headmaster saw that I had grown too attached to the creature, to the point that I was losing focused. He took my lizard companion away from me but he promised he would find someone at Diamondvale to take care of it.

After receiving his assurance, I began the experiment with Subject D as I promised. I re-synthesized the Geode-stone compound and gave it to Subject D. There were no immediate effects that day.

Day 134

After a month of monitoring and little change, I was about to give up on Subject D. However, as I was about to throw in the towel, the subject transformed. His metamorphosis was nothing I had ever seen before. His whole physique had changed as he was way taller and stronger than before. But none of that compared to his most lethal arsenal, his deathly wail.

Day 154

It has been awhile but Headmaster Volice showed up today to view the results of Subject D. He was in high spirits to see that the experiment had progressed and he asked when the final concoction would be ready. I was honest with him and told him that much testing still needed to be done. There were too many unreliable side-effects on Subject D such as lack of control and loss of human sanity.

He was disheartened by what I reported, but he raised two fingers on his right hand. He told me that he would only wait for two more positive trial runs before performing the operation.

Day 172

Subject D continues to slam his cage and unleash his wailing. I want to release him out into the wilds where he wouldn't have to endure any more testing, but I don't know how he will fair out in Nadir. Although he is a big creature, deep down he is a sensitive soul.

In addition to keeping tabs on Subject D, I have also made many discoveries on the Geode-stones. The microscope I have used detected chemical structures within these crystals that can affect one's memory. In their solid state, these chemicals are inactive, but once they are turned into other states, the effects can vary. I'm already aware of students at

Diamondvale who have used Geode-breaker and don't have any recollection of doing so.

However, I have a feeling the effects can be far more potent when transformed into vapour form. If my hypothesis is correct, the great city of Zenith, which releases Geode-stone residue into Nadir, not only affects the breathing conditions of its inhabitants but their memories as well. It would explain how I couldn't recognize anyone who arrived at the lab that day.

Day 200

Subject D has been growing more violent and I don't think the cage will hold him for long. Headmaster Volice ordered me to create a device that would better restrain him. I obeyed his orders but there are bigger issues I want to discuss as this could be my final entry.

I can feel my memory fading from all the Geode-stone residue from Zenith. I don't have much recollection of the majority of my time here. The only thing that kept my faint memories alive is that I have been writing as frequently as I could. I realize there is vital information within this logbook that could be useful for others outside the confines of this lab.

I'm taking a big chance, but I trust this book will fall into the hands of the right people. Someone, please find us and save these subjects from further pain and suffering.

Signed, Doctor Vihaan.

After Doctor Vihaan finished writing his last entry, he got a raven to take the book, hoping it would deliver it to someone who could help. The raven went through a tough journey and would eventually drop the book in the hands of Professor Rice who was hiding out in Nadir helping Devan and Dante recover from their injuries.

While Dante still required more time to get used to his new mechanical body, he tasked Devan with infiltrating Zenith and getting the book into the archives where he had a feeling one of the students within Diamondvale would find it.

The Shadow Courier

Myla hadn't been gone for more than a month but Sahil had already managed to find a new tenant. He never saw this new tenant often but she was able to make her first payment, which gave assurance to Sahil. As he was counting his profits, Jacob entered the inn.

"For the twentieth time, she isn't here! Man, you are one persistent fellow. Shouldn't you be guarding the gate?"

Jacob gave Sahil a look and when the Innkeeper saw, he apologized to everyone in the dining hall that the business was closed early for maintenance. People were disappointed as some of them made their way to their room, while others left the Inn.

"Seriously Sahil, there are no other leads, it has to be her. Tell me where she is."

"Jacob, I don't know. This new tenant of mine rarely shows up! I'm not even sure why she pays for the place!"

"And that doesn't make you the least suspicious?"

"Hey, business is business. I don't judge!"

Jacob was unamused, he asked Sahil for the keys to the tenant's room. Sahil rejected the idea stating that it would be an invasion of privacy. Jacob raised his eyebrow at Sahil and eventually, he caved in. He was too curious and wanted to know what his mysterious tenant was up to.

Once they made their way to the room, Sahil pulled out the key and unlocked the door. He slowly turned the doorknob, bracing himself for what he might see. When they entered the room, they found nothing out of the ordinary.

"Ugh! I can't believe I let you talk me into doing this Jacob! She's just a normal client who..."

"Let's search the place, it looks, too normal..." Jacob responded.

"Too normal? What kind of reasoning is that?!" He was frustrated. "Fine, we'll do a quick search but if we find nothing, I'm never listening to you again!"

They had been searching for some time but they couldn't find anything suspicious. The frustration within Sahil was building up until he spotted something that caught his eye.

"This can't be... This is the best candy ever and I haven't had it in years!" They were orange and yellow and covered in sugar.

"No way, they're the fuzzy ones! Hey, give me some!" Jacob yelled.

They were about to fight over a piece of candy when they suddenly heard a noise coming from the door. The doorknob turned and it was beginning to open.

Jacob and Sahil were now panicking and they immediately ran into the other room. When they opened the door and jumped into the room, they found themselves stuck against something.

"What the? What is this stuff?" Jacob asked.

"It can't be... tape?!"

Sahil was shocked the room was filled with tape for security purposes. They struggled to break free but the tape was far tougher than they thought. With the sound of the door opening, they both sealed their lips and hoped for a way out of their predicament.

Entering the room was a girl who wore glasses and stood no taller than five feet. She looked around the room and she noticed something was different. It was clear to her that someone had entered into her unit. Slowly, she made her way towards her room.

Jacob and Sahil continued to be silent as they could hear the footsteps closing in. The tenant was reaching for the door and all they could do was brace themselves as they were about to be caught.

However, a loud ticking sound coming from the window caught her attention.

A crow was pecking at the window and the tenant immediately allowed it inside. The feathered animal then made some crow noises that sounded like gibberish. When it finished, it flew out of the room. The girl followed after the crow, after grabbing a leather pouch on the table.

With her gone, Jacob and Sahil were allowed to move and make noises again. It took a while, but after much struggle and a hint of teamwork, they untangled themselves from the room of tape with Sahil fell onto the ground.

"Come on, let's get going," Jacob spoke.

Sahil looked out the window and saw no sight of the tenant or the crow. She also did a good job leaving no trail behind for others to track her. She was more sly and cunning than she appeared to be.

"Looks like we have no leads to go on. Let's head back and forget that ever happened!"

"It's okay, I know where she is going," Jacob responded.

"What? How?" Sahil was shocked until he remembered that one of the things Jacob learned as a gatekeeper was communicating with birds. He understood what the crow had said.

"Follow me."

The girl made her way to the hidden underpass within Nadir. When she arrived, she found herself alone holding the contraband stashed away inside a coin pouch. She held onto it tightly, knowing this area was filled with people who didn't go by any particular rules.

It didn't take long before a gang of punk-looking guys showed up and scattered through the area. The girl stood her ground and showed the pouch to them. She threatened that she would drop the contraband down the sewers if they moved any closer.

Her threats worked as they all stood still in their position. Then she heard someone clapping their hands approaching her way.

"Your reputation precedes you, Shadow Courier."

Hiding in the alleyway and spying on the conversation were Jacob and Sahil. When Sahil heard the title of his tenant, his expression changed but Jacob was clueless.

Sahil told Jacob that the 'Shadow Courier' was a legend amongst merchants and business owners. This person was known for their incredible skill in smuggling illegal goods and trading them for an incredible return.

"That little girl is the legendary Shadow Courier?!" Jacob was in disbelief but Sahil just shrugged his shoulders. He told Jacob to keep quiet and listen.

"You must be the leader of these hooligans." Her words irritated the man's minions and they were ready to attack her but the leader held them back.

"Do you have the goods?"

The Shadow Courier held out the pouch that was in her hands. He demanded for her to reveal the contents within. She was annoyed, but she pulled the string and out of the pouch was the contraband she smuggled, Geode-stones.

The kingpin reached out towards the crystals but the girl pulled them away. She would not allow him to get near without giving her payment first. The big man had a dissatisfied look. He snapped his finger and one of his lackeys returned with a briefcase.

The minion opened it up and after seeing the contents revealed, the Shadow Courier was pleased. She received the briefcase before exchanging it for the pouch of Geode-stones. The instant the trade was complete, she was ready to flee the scene.

"Well, it was nice doing business with you. Now we can just go our separate ways and..." Her path was blocked as the minions stood in her way.

The kingpin grabbed one of the Geode-stones and held it with one hand. All his underlings were filled with anticipation as he was about to break the gem.

Jacob couldn't wait any longer. The situation had gotten worse and he was ready to intervene. But again, Sahil told Jacob to wait.

The Geode-stone was crushed by the boss but nothing happened. All his henchmen were confused until one of them took a Geode-stone from the pouch and put it in his mouth.

"Hey! This tastes like... Candy!"

The leader was furious as he gave a malicious stare to the notorious girl. The Shadow Courier waved nervously, hoping to calm him down.

"Get her."

As all the lackeys darted towards her, Jacob was about to step out of hiding but Sahil continued to hold him back. They argued for a moment before they saw what was about to happen.

Because of her tiny stature, the shifty rogue was extremely nimble. Two henchmen from opposite sides attempted to grab her but she ducked, allowing the two men to collide against each other.

Another goon appeared after, hoping to catch her by surprise, but she cart-wheeled out of the way and he ran into a wall. Then she appeared before another crony, who went for a bear hug but she slid through between his legs.

She was now running towards the exit but one underling stood in her way. He thought he had the girl where he wanted her. However, from underneath her sleeves, two strands of tape flew out and latched onto a high surface nearby. She pulled herself up and swung passed the enemy who blocked her path.

The kingpin saw the Shadow Courier escaping through the secret tunnel underneath that led to the outskirts of Nadir. He called for his remaining flunkies to follow him as he was not letting the pipsqueak go after she made a mockery out of him. He and two of his followers managed to make it through but blocking the rest off was Jacob.

The gatekeeper of Nadir took out a couple of henchmen easily which caught the attention of the rest. Despite being outnumbered six to one, Jacob was ready to fight on with his spear in hand, but suddenly Sahil appeared.

"Seriously? You are going to tell me to wait again?"

"Nah, I think you should go after the Shadow Courier and the kingpin."

Jacob was shocked by Sahil's words as the innkeeper urged him to leave before he lost their trail. The gatekeeper thanked Sahil and he left to pursue his targets, leaving the lonely innkeeper to deal with the remaining goons.

The flunkies were all laughing as they thought they had an easy victory. However, little did they know, some of Sahil's memories had returned when he saw the fake Geode-stones. He pulled out a weapon that resembled the shape of a hockey stick, which felt very natural to him. He took off his glasses and told his opponents, "Two minutes, that is all I will need."

Unlikely Allies

After escaping the underpass area in Nadir, the Shadow Courier felt she could finally relax. She was walking towards her hideout which was located just outside the boundaries of the Polluted Wilds. Although that would seem dangerous to most, to her it was perfect as that meant there would be fewer visitors.

When she arrived at the entrance of her hideout, she called for someone. "Hey, it's safe to come out!" There was no reply. "I got you your favourite..." She held out a piece of candy to entice the creature to come out. "Oh come on! Stop being a scaredy cat you..."

She became vigilant after hearing a noise near her vicinity. However, it was too late as two of the henchmen managed to sneak up on the Shadow Courier and pin her down. She kept squirming in hopes of breaking free but she could not. As she continued to struggle, the kingpin stood in front of her.

"I normally don't deal kindly to people who double-cross me. However, I'm feeling generous today. Give me the Geode-stones..."

"Wow, are you daft? I don't have any! I never did!"

He was not pleased with her answer. Now that he found out the Shadow Courier lied, he wanted retribution. He was ready to unleash his full wrath on the girl but a bolt of lightning struck his two lackeys that were holding down the rogue.

The kingpin looked back and was shocked to see Jacob the gatekeeper this far out of Nadir. He reached for his brass knuckles and secured them on his hands. His knuckles were ready to make contact against the gatekeeper but Jacob sidestepped the attack and then used the shaft of his spear to trip the kingpin.

Jacob had no intention of fighting the leader, as his focus was on the Shadow Courier. He ignored the big man lying on the floor and went straight to the little con artist.

"Oh thank you for saving me from that mean nasty old man!" She tried to sound all innocent.

"Drop the act. I know who you are, Shadow Courier."

"Who's that? Never heard of it. My name is Keira, and I'm just an innocent harmless girl."

As the boss got back to his feet, he was very annoyed with the fact that his presence was being ignored. "HEY! What are you two doing?! Don't you know I'm still here!?"

"I can deal with you later. You are honestly pretty weak." Jacob insulted the man.

"Haha! Ouch, that must sting!" Keira added salt to the wound.

Not happy about the fact that he seemed insignificant, he ran with fervor attempting to show them both his true strength. As he was in mid-air, both Jacob and Keira simultaneously threw a kick without even looking and sent the egotistical man on his back. Without skipping a beat they continued their argument.

"Hand it over!" Jacob demanded.

"What?"

"You know what I'm talking about. The Geode-stones!"

"Why does everyone think I have them? Sheesh, no wonder it's so easy to rip people off."

"Listen, those Geode-stones are very dangerous and you are putting yourself in a lot of danger if you hang onto them."

"For the last time, I don't have any! Gosh, you people are so stubborn!"

Jacob was about to lose his patience and drag Keira back to Nadir by force. However, the kingpin had gotten up and he was standing near his lackeys who were still unconscious. Despite looking beat up, he wanted their attention.

"Oh, it's just you again. I'll arrest you another time. Now run away before I change my mind."

Jacob's comment fell on deaf ears as the man reached for something in his coat. It was a vial that contained a mysterious liquid. Keira couldn't have cared less about the content but when Jacob saw it, some memories appeared in his mind. It was telling him the mixtures contained essence from the Geode-stones.

"I was hoping to get more of this stuff before using it. Let's see if what the old man said is true." The kingpin began administering the vial to his two underlings.

Jacob yelled for the man to stop but it was too late. His two henchmen had received the mixture and their bodies began to transform. Standing before Jacob and Keira were two mindless Geode-Mutants.

Jacob tried to warn Keira about the mutants but she ran circles around the creatures while wrapping them up with her strands of tape. With the mutant unable to move, she threw a punch right at the lower abdomen but it had no effect. The mutants used their claw to cut free of the tape and they now had their sights set on Keira who hurt her hand.

Luckily, Jacob jumped in and drove his spear into the creature's shoulder. He then kicked Keira out of the way and pulled his weapon out, before separating from the mutant.

"What are those things?"

Jacob didn't have an answer but the kingpin did. "Haha! These monsters are known as Geode-Mutants and they will be your demise! Get them!"

Despite his command, his once loyal henchmen didn't respond. "Didn't you hear me? I said..."

The Geode-Mutant near him grabbed him by the throat. The man who was once the superior was now begging for his mutated underling to let him go. The creature complied by throwing his former master hard against a tree and he lost all movement throughout his body.

Seeing how strong the mutants were, Jacob wasn't inclined to stay any longer. He planned to flee but Keira would not allow it.

"No, not yet! We can't leave!"

"What is it now?"

"My friend, he's still in the cave!"

"Oh, you mean your cat?"

"Yeah, kind of."

"You are a real piece of work. Fine, I will stall for as long as I can. Hurry up and get your kitty."

"Wait, he's..."

Before Keira could explain, Jacob charged toward the two Geode-Mutants. He went straight for his signature lightning strike that chained against both his targets. They were electrocuted but somehow after only a few seconds, they were able to move again.

Seeing that his lightning strike had little effect, he changed strategies and went for a melee attack. His spear made contact with one of his enemies but when he tried to retrieve his weapon, the mutant grabbed hold. The other one tackled him and then sent him to the ground. As Jacob slowly got back up, he saw Keira beside him.

"Why are you still here? You are supposed to get your cat!"

"Yeah... About that..."

The mutants both growled and interrupted their conversation. Jacob was now unarmed and they had nowhere to run but suddenly, something hit the side of the Geode-mutant's head.

They saw rocks flying at bullet speed. When Jacob turned to where the projectiles were coming from, he saw Sahil launching the rocks like a puck with a hockey stick. The Geode-Mutants had to cover themselves as Sahil continued his barrage. That created enough of a distraction for Jacob to grab his spear and charge up for one final attack. He gathered all the energy he had and channelled it into his spear. His weapon burst with lightning energy and he directed all of it towards the Geode-Mutants. The attack successfully landed and their enemies were defeated.

"You seriously had trouble with those weak creatures? I thought the gatekeepers were stronger than that." Sahil wasn't too impressed.

"Hey, it was my attack just now that finished them off!"

While they were disputing, Keira was quietly trying to slip away. When she took her first tip-toe step, a rock flew just short of her foot.

"And where do you think you are going?" Sahil deliberately missed his last shot.

"Umm, anywhere but here?" She said nervously.

Sahil was ready to fire another rock at the girl to interrogate her but Jacob held him back. "It's alright Sahil, she doesn't have the Geode-stones. We can let her go."

"What? You mean we did all that work for nothing?!" Sahil dropped down in disappointment.

"So I can just leave? No strings attached." Keira asked.

"Just go before I change my mind."

"You got it, mister! I will be out of your..."

Before she could leave, they could hear a growling sound coming from multiple directions. They banded together as they saw a horde of Geode-Mutants emerging from the shadows. Then, the original two that they thought were defeated, were also back on their feet.

They were surrounded, and their options were limited. Keira's tape wouldn't have much effect on the mutants, Jacob's energy was drained from using his lightning strike and Sahil was running out of ammunition as well. With nowhere to run, they stood their ground hoping to make the best with what they had.

The Geode-Mutants were a foot away from reaching their targets but they heard a noise coming from the cave. It sounded like a creature running towards them but judging from the sound it was making, it was too large to be a cat. Pouncing out of the cave was a crystalized lion.

It crashed, knocking away three Geode-Mutants before unleashing a deafening roar.

"Leo!" Keira shouted in excitement.

That was when Jacob put it all together. "That is your cat?!"

By himself, Leo fought back the Geode-mutants and they were sent flying against the ground. They were relentless as they all could get back up but when Leo took a breath in and unleashed his roar that could be heard throughout the forest, the creatures froze in their spot. They turned around and walked away from Jacob, Keira, and Sahil.

"Leo, you did it!" She gave the beast a hug for his efforts.

"This whole time you had a lion hiding in there?! Why didn't you tell me sooner!"

As Jacob yelled, Leo gave a small roar and frightened him. He was so startled that he ran behind Sahil for cover.

Keira held the lion back, letting them know the two people before her were her allies. "I tried to tell you but you wouldn't listen!"

"Keep him away from me!"

"Oh, come on Jacob, don't tell me you are scared of that cat."

"I'm not scared!"

Suddenly there was the sound of steps walking on tree branches that startled Jacob again. Keira and Sahil were both struck with fear as well, thinking that Geode-Mutants had returned. Leo jumped to the front again, ready to fend off the mindless creatures but emerging from the forest was someone they weren't expecting.

"Hey guys."

"Devan?" Jacob somehow recognized him.

New Plan

With a good chunk of their former class reunited, some of their memories were starting to come back but there was still much missing. Many of them would have welcomed a formal reunion but that would have to wait. There were many pressing matters for them to tackle.

First, on their list, many of them were injured and needed medical attention. Immediately, Doctor Ashima came to mind for Rice but when he brought up her name, everyone shrivelled in fear. She was one of the people they needed to rescue, along with a couple others that came to Myla's attention.

"Jacob and Sahil! They are still in Nadir! We have to go get them before..." Her body started to ache before she could finish. Most of them were in similar condition as Myla after the damage they suffered against Headmaster Volice.

Rice quickly deduced the situation and assigned Devan to go locate Sahil and Jacob. Myla was still worried but Rice had faith that the two back in Nadir could handle themselves.

That left the most pressing matter: finding the lab and stopping Volice. They were all at a loss about how to proceed. Even Harshitha and Netanya who normally had brilliant schemes were silent. They also couldn't rely on Dante as his systems were severely damaged after the battle. It seemed they were at an impasse until Rice spoke up.

He told them to focus on recovering from their injuries first. It didn't make sense for them to stress about anything else until they were in fighting shape. Everyone felt relaxed after hearing him say those words. However, one of the group members noticed that Rice wasn't staying to rest with them.

"Hey! Where are you going?" Aria shouted.

"To the hidden lab of course!"

"What? You know where it is?!" Netanya asked in surprise.

"Of course I do." He smiled.

"Why didn't you just say so? Come on everyone let's all..."

Before Arnav could finish his sentence, Rice shocked everyone when he replied, "No." It was only for a split second, but everyone felt a tremendous force pressing against their body. For a moment, they had an idea of the strength he had been suppressing around them.

When he had their attention, he explained that he would go on ahead and do what he could to slow down the Headmaster's ploy.

"Sure, but there is still one problem. We don't know where or how to get to the place without you!" Harshitha emphasized.

Rice looked to Willyham. "Ask him. He knows the way."

Everyone turned their focus to Willyham who looked confused. "Huh, what?"

Seeing Willyham clueless, they looked back to Rice but he had disappeared from their sight.

Everyone was frustrated as they couldn't believe they had fallen for his trick. Now they were stuck without any leads on how to reach Volice's hidden lab. Disagreement was about to break loose until Netanya had a thought.

"Wait! Maybe he didn't trick us."

"Netanya, do you really think Willyham knows?" Harshitha asked skeptically.

"Sorry Netanya but I got nothing," Willyham admitted.

"That's because we all thought he was talking about Willyham, but Rice was actually speaking to Willyham!" Everyone looked confused so Netanya elaborated. "Willyham, Rice was talking about Barmaan! Where is he?"

"Oh, I left him back at our classroom."

"Alright everyone, get some rest. Tomorrow, we break into our former school." Arnav announced.

Break Through

Entering the city of Zenith were the group of former students of Diamondvale, now deemed outlaws. Netanya, Harshitha, Arnav, Ajay and Willyham all had their wrist in shackles as Captain Saivik took the front and Enforcer Max was at the rear. Saivik guided them towards the entrance of Diamondvale with the crowd watching the scene and whispering rumours to one another.

Moving through the marketplace area, the prisoners were followed closely by a merchant hauling his supplies on his wagon covered by a giant cloth. He even had a monkey on his back as they were heading towards Diamondvale.

When Saivik arrived at the gate of Diamondvale with the fugitives, he was met with a couple of enforcers guarding the front entrance. The private was excited to see the return of his captain and he began asking questions in quick succession.

Saivik let the excited enforcer know that he was on a time crunch and he needed to get the prisoners into confinement immediately. The private snapped out of his excitement and allowed his captain to proceed with Max. The rookie enforcer gave the signal to allow safe passage of entry.

Once Saivik, Max and all the convicts entered the Diamondvale premise, the enforcer saw the next person in line, the merchant with the monkey and his wagon. At the same time, a group of enforcers appeared out of hiding and surrounded Saivik, Max and the former students of Diamondvale.

"What is the meaning of this? I am your captain and I demand you let me through!" Saivik raised his voice.

"Sorry captain, but your rankings have been revoked." One of the enforcers held out a poster that showed the captain and Max had been deemed traitors. The enforcers thought they had Saivik and Max outnumbered until they heard a loud screech coming from the monkey. Sarmaan's warcry was the signal to let everyone know that the first phase of the plan was over.

Liam took off the cloth from the wagon. Jumping out were Aria, Myla and Dante who surprised the enforcers. While they kept initial forces busy, Saivik and Max broke the shackles off everyone else so they could all join the fight.

With their combined efforts, they were able to defeat the first wave of enforcers but reinforcements were on their way. Myla, Dante, Ajay, Arnav, and Netanya stayed to hold off the oncoming forces. The rest separated into two groups to carry out their mission.

Ashima was walking through the hospital, about to see her next patient. She was stopped by a couple of enforcers who had an important request for her. The doctor was annoyed but she agreed to follow the guards.

After taking a few steps, Sarmaan broke through the hospital window in his gorilla form. He grabbed both enforcers and tossed them aside. That alerted a small group of security guards, who were making their way to apprehend the gorilla.

While Ashima was confused and trying to make sense of the situation, Sarmaan grabbed the doctor by the waist and ran from the guards. The group of enforcers also joined in to pursue after the crystal gorilla but a torrential wave rushed down the corridor and washed them away. Harshitha had appeared to help with the rescue.

Sarmaan kept running as fast as he could but when he arrived at a fork in the hallway, he saw enforcers running at him from all directions.

"Hey, what are you doing? Put me down!" Ashima was punching Sarmaan's back. She continued to struggle until she saw Harshitha appear next to her. "Harshitha? What are you doing here? I thought you were all healed!"

"It's a bit complicated but we are here to rescue you."

"Rescue me? From what? I'm not in any danger! Do you know this crazy gorilla? Tell him to put me down!"

Harshitha paused for a moment to think carefully about her next move. She swung her orb towards Sarmaan but at the last moment, she changed the trajectory and bonked Ashima in the head, causing her to fall unconscious. Sarmaan thanked Harshitha for making his job easier but they still had to find a way out of their predicament.

Harshitha and Sarmaan were ready to bash their way through but coming down one of the halls was a barrel that rolled towards one group of enforcers. They looked closely and saw a lit fuse that was about to detonate a huge barrel of explosives. Sarmaan and Harshitha jumped for cover and the explosion sent the enforcers flying through the halls.

When the smoke cleared, the gorilla and the student saw Liam at the end of the hallway. He told them both to follow him as more guards were on their way. They ran with the pirate until they arrived at a dead end in the hospital. They were about to turn back but they could hear footsteps rushing towards their direction.

"You led us to a dead end! What were you thinking?!" As Harshitha was yelling, Liam pointed to the window.

"You are going to use the zipline to get out!" He said with excitement.

Harshitha looked out the window and stared down from where they were. "Uh... is there another..." jumping on the zipline with reckless abandon was Sarmaan who hung on and slid down the line with the unconscious Ashima. When he made it down to the bottom, he turned back and gave a big thumbs-up.

"Ok, your turn!" shouted Liam.

"I... umm... don't like heights."

"You what?!" Liam couldn't believe what he was hearing. Harshitha, one of the highest-ranking students had a common fear just like a regular person. He felt some empathy for her but the feeling faded as the mass of enforcers had spotted them.

Liam forced Harshitha out the window and then the zipline. He told her to hold on as he was getting ready to push her.

"Wait, what about you?"

"I'll be right behind you!" He pushed Harshitha who screamed the entire way down the line.

Harshitha was going too fast and she would have face-planted on the ground but Sarmaan caught her in time. She thanked the gorilla for saving her and then she turned around hoping to see Liam right behind her but he never appeared.

Back up top in the hospital, Liam turned around to face the oncoming enforcers. He was no match for their combined strength but he had one stick of dynamite in his hand. He threw it to the side, completely missing all his enemies.

They all laughed at his terrible aim until they realized where the dynamite landed. There were dozens of barrels loaded with explosives. The enforcers all scrambled in hopes to escape but it was too late. The barrels detonated, causing an explosion on the entire floor. Luckily, it was a floor where there were no patients. The only ones caught in the blast were the bulk of the enforcers and Liam.

Sarmaan and Harshitha looked on from the outside. They could hear the sound of the walls being blown up and windows shattering. Rain began to fall heavily from the sky but more importantly, tears flowed from both their eyes.

"Come on Sarmaan. Let's leave before they find us."

Sarmaan had lost his dear friend but he knew they had to press forward or else Liam's sacrifice would have been in vain.

Infiltrating Willyham's old classroom were Aria, Max, Saivik, and Willyham. This area was not filled with enforcers but it was easy to get lost. Thankfully, Saivik and Max had most of the place memorized.

There hadn't been much resistance on their adventure so far until a couple of emerald-ranked students appeared to block their way. Aria and Max were ready to fight but Saivik stepped in front of them and told them to move ahead.

Aria and Max took Willyham and went on their way. Saivik turned his attention to the two emerald-ranked students who looked the same. Saivik drew his electrically charged staff out and clashed against his two opponents, each holding a small crystal dagger.

Max, Aria, and Willyham continued through the school grounds, inching closer to the classroom. They had a solid pace but falling from the ceiling was a large student who was about to crush Willyham. Luckily, Aria managed to push him out of harm's way.

As the enormous student was recovering from the impact, Aria signalled for the two boys to move on ahead. They both understood their assignment and went on without her. Aria then turned to face her opponent. When the dust settled, Aria saw a student who towered over her with a diamond insignia on his uniform. She was about to square off against an opponent who was even taller than her, holding a giant crystal-wrecking ball tied to a chain.

"Today is your lucky day because you get to face the strongest student in Diamondvale!" Despite his boasting and his stature, Aria was not impressed.

Not getting the reaction he wanted, he whirled his weapon in the air and then threw it in Aria's direction. She was able to dodge the initial impact but as the ball struck the ground, debris scattered and some of it flew towards Aria, leaving cuts on her arms and her face. The student followed up by grabbing the chain and pulling it back, retracting the wrecking ball towards him and hitting Aria on its way back.

The collision knocked Aria to the ground and he boasted about his strength. His confidence was at a high, thinking his opponent had been defeated, but Aria refused to quit. As she was fixing her stance and cracking her neck, memories of her training in the Amazon Borderlands and Diamondvale surged through her mind.

With her hands, she provoked her opponent to attack her again. He didn't hold back as he swung his weapon with great strength. Again, Aria dodged the first strike but instead of the debris damaging her body, she swatted it away with her gauntlets and blitzed at her enemy.

The man was surprised by Aria's speed and he began to sweat. He pulled the chain as quickly as he could and the wrecking ball was going to retract and squish Aria on the second attempt.

It was about an inch away from making contact against Aria but at the last moment, she did a flip and barely evaded the weapon. Now the wrecking ball was heading towards its owner at high velocity. The student had no time to dodge, so he was forced to hold his ground and use his hands to push back the wrecking ball. He managed to slow it down but he wasn't expecting what was about to happen next.

Aria, launched herself full force and punched the wrecking ball with her dominant fist. Her momentum and power added to the force of the wrecking ball, leaving her opponent completely overwhelmed. Not only was he pushed back, but his feet dug into the ground as they were dragged across the floor. Eventually, the force pushed him against the walls of the building and he was nearly squished by his weapon.

The only reason he was still breathing was because Aria held back. Some of his bones were fractured, some broken and it was clear he could no longer continue the fight. He conceded the battle and Aria walked away without saying another word.

Max and Willyham weren't too far from the classroom where Barmaan's cage was but Max suddenly stopped. Willyham was confused as to why but the enforcer simply told Willyham that the classroom wasn't too far away.

When asked by Willyham where he was going, Max wasn't very detailed in his answer. "There is something I must take care of." He turned back in the opposite direction and Willyham had no choice but to find Barmaan all by himself.

Returning to the battle between the captain and the two identical-looking students, Saivik seemed to have things under control. He had both his enemies breathing heavily and he wasn't breaking a sweat.

"Wow, they will let anyone into emerald rank these days." Saivik taunted.

That was when his opponent decided to get serious. Suddenly one of the emerald students disappeared.

"Eh, what happened to your twin?"

"I have no twin brother."

"Huh? Then who was that just now?"

Saivik's opponent pulled out his Geode-stone and placed it onto his weapon. He explained his special ability known as the 'mirror blade.' Essentially he could make a copy of himself to help him fight. When he finished explaining, Saivik was no longer dealing with one opponent but at least twenty.

In unison, they all jumped at him. Saivik managed to repel back four of the clones but there were too many of them. He became overpowered by their sheer numbers and was beaten to the ground.

"It appears the great captain of the enforcers is finished. You ain't all you are hyped up to be."

Somehow, Saivik managed to stand up. As he was regaining some of his memories, he began to remove the sleeve on his right hand and something was attached to his wrist.

"Did you know I was given a nickname before becoming captain of the enforcers?"

"We could care less but go ahead, amuse us." Replied one of the clones.

"It's shooter. Shooter Saivik."

Immediately after saying it, he held out his right arm and the contraption on his wrist activated. A couple of clips opened up from the side making it look like a mini-crossbow. He had a Geode-stone powering it up and in an instant, a laser shot out of it and vaporized one of the clones.

All the other clones reacted by charging towards Saivik but none of them would be able to touch him. The captain had found his rhythm. He would roll away to create separation between them and take out about two clones each time. This pattern repeated until there was only one enemy left. He begged for mercy and Saivik shot him right in the side of his shoulder.

The wound caused his opponent much pain but he would survive. Saivik was about to walk away but his opponent called for him.

"Tell me, why did you become a traitor against the school."

"I'm not a traitor."

"Tch, exactly what a traitor would say."

"Whatever, that is your opinion. I'm sorry you can't see the truth."

"And I'm sorry too." He replied with a grim tone to Saivik.

"Huh? Why would you be..." Suddenly the opponent he was talking to disappeared. Saivik realized at that moment, that the real enemy was still out there. In a panic, he frantically looked around hoping to spot him, but it was too late. He felt something strike him on the back and when he looked down at his ribs, he saw a blade pierced through the left side. Saivik was now down on his knees.

"Oh captain... you thought it would be that easy?"

Saivik fired another laser and struck his target, but it was another clone that evaporated and another appeared to take its place.

"I know better than to take you in a direct fight. You can't get to the higher ranks in Diamondvale on pure muscle alone, you need intelligence."

Saivik was struggling to sit up as his strength was fading.

"I will give you credit where it's due. You lasted much longer than any of my other opponents, but your time is over."

As his clone raised its blade, he noticed the captain still smiling. "What's so funny?"

"Because you are so convinced you have won."

"But I have!" He hesitated.

"You think I don't know who you are? As captain of the enforcers, I have information on every student at Diamondvale. I was aware of your ability and fighting strategies the moment this fight began."

The clone maker was nervous but he tried to hide it. "It doesn't matter! You have no idea where I am and there's no way for you to reach me!"

"You are hiding in the clock tower across from us," Saivik replied with confidence.

"What?! How..."

"I had you figured out from the start. You are right about one thing though, I can't get to you. But he can."

Standing on the rooftops was Max holding out a bow with an arrow. He could see his target on the other side. He released the arrow towards the clock tower and hit his target. All the clones that were near Saivik, all simultaneously evaporated into thin air.

Willyham was now entering his old classroom. As he opened the door, he saw nobody else inside other than a crystal lizard in his cage. Willyham ran up to Barmaan but someone appeared to block his way.

"Oh hi, Professor Sam! Fancy bumping into you here."

"Willyham, this is my classroom."

"Oh yeah, I knew that, I just wanted to stop by and say hi."

He was nervous and lying. Sam approached him ominously and stared him eye to eye.

"Willyham, tell me the truth. Why are you here?"

He took a deep breath before speaking.

"Professor Sam, I don't know what is happening! Everything started great, Netanya and Ajay have been kind to me, showing me around Diamondvale. I got to meet stronger fighters like Arnav and Harshitha through them. Then suddenly my two friends disappeared. Harshitha grabs me and tells me to be quiet. Next thing I know, she is busting out the intruder and we're under attack by the enforcers. We then see Headmaster Volice who is so strong and beats up everyone just by staring at them. But then some mysterious man shows up to stop Volice. I'm finding out that I might not be a new student at this school and I'm working with people whom I thought I never met before but they might be my friends from another time at Diamondvale. And now we are working together to stop Volice!"

When he finished, he felt a huge relief as he sat down with his head over his arms and began to cry. He had been overwhelmed for so long and he finally had a chance to release his emotions.

Professor Sam who listened to him, slowly approached him. When Willyham heard her footsteps, his heart sank. He wasn't sure what his teacher would do to him, so he continued to cover his eyes.

She stopped and seemed ready to pull out her weapon but barging into the room was a group of enforcers.

"Professor! Allow us to take care of the rest."

The enforcers made their way towards Willyham who was now scared out of his mind. He didn't know what to do but what kept him going was the thought that everyone was risking their life for him to grab Barmaan.

He had a sudden burst of energy and was ready to fight but when he opened his eyes, he saw all the enforcers defeated. The only one standing was Professor Sam.

"Professor Sam, did you...?"

She didn't answer. Instead, she took Barmaan out of his cage and put him in Willyham's hands. "Go."

He wiped his tears and accepted the lizard. "Thank you, Professor Sam! I won't let you down!" She smiled as she watched her student running out of the classroom.

Returning near the entrance of Diamondvale, Myla, Dante, Ajay and Netanya were standing their ground against the enforcers. They had been stalling for a great length of time and finally, they could see both groups returning. They only had to hold out a little longer.

Netanya waved her wand and created a bubble forcefield to keep the enemy at bay. Sarmaan carried Ashima out with Saivik, Willyham, Max, and Ajay following after.

The enforcers continuously tried to disrupt the forcefield and eventually, they were able to break through. Netanya had expended much of her energy and the enemies were about to apprehend her.

Jumping in to kick a few of them aside was Myla, followed by a flurry of punches from Aria. They stood ready to take on the mass of Diamondvale's security but an electrical barrier appeared with Arnav standing behind it.

Dante told both Myla and Aria to take Netanya to safety first. He assured them that he and Arnav would have the situation under control. So the two women picked up Netanya and escaped together.

The enforcers attempted to chase after everyone but Arnav charged forward with his shield in front and Dante gave him supporting fire.

They successfully repelled all the enforcers but a group of bloodhounds were running towards them. They slipped past Arnav's defence, leaving Dante vulnerable.

As the hounds pounced they were knocked aside by a floating orb. It swiftly ricocheted between all the bloodhounds, leaving Dante unscathed. When Arnav saw the weapon, he knew who had arrived.

"Harshitha!" He was excited to see her but taking a closer look into her eyes, he realized something terrible must have happened. He was about to ask but she gave a swift reply. "Go!" Arnav grabbed Dante and they left immediately.

Harshitha turned to face the remaining army heading her way. Although their numbers had been reduced by a significant amount, there were still plenty.

The mass of enforcers thought they had her beat but Harshitha wasn't holding back any longer. She raised her right hand and a torrential wave appeared that towered over all her enemies. They all stopped as they were mesmerized by the sight of her power. She then dropped down her arm and the wave came crashing down.

It forced the enforcers to scatter in hopes of avoiding the raging water but they would all be swallowed up and washed away. With her enemies defeated, Harshitha walked away, leaving Diamondvale and Zenith to catch up with her friends.

Friends or Foes

S ome of the memories had returned to Devan and Jacob about their past life in Zenith. They were so excited to see each other that they began acting very immaturely. They were performing secret high fives and making random warcry that no one else could understand.

Keira was speechless at what she witnessed. She looked to Leo who shrugged his shoulders. They both looked to Sahil who pretended that he had no idea who the two were.

They continued their comical act until a haunting wail echoed through the wilds. Instantly, they all readied themselves for what was about to approach them. It was the towering Geode-Mutant beast and along with a mass of lesser minions.

Sahil, Jacob and Devan were prepared to fight. They were thinking they could take the beast if they all attacked together but Keira had other ideas.

"Oh no, I'm done with this place!" She hopped onto Leo's back.

"What? You little... You can't just chicken out like that!" Devan was ready to give her a full-on lecture but Jacob stepped in. He let Devan know that she was free to make her own choice.

There was a brief pause before Keira commanded Leo to leave the area. They fled, leaving the three men to battle against the beast and the army of mindless Geode-Mutants.

T he large group that left Zenith was now in Nadir. They made their way swiftly through the area hoping to reach the Polluted Wild without delay. Barmaan was leading the way with everyone following close behind.

They all halted their advance when they felt a strong gust of wind blow by them. There was a blur circling them for a moment and then it slowed down. Myla immediately recognized the Geode-Mutant Beast from their encounter at the Amazon Borderlands.

She elected to stay behind to battle the creature. Ajay and Saivik volunteered to help, while everyone else continued on their way.

Their foe was not large in stature but Myla warned her allies that their opponent was incredibly fast. Together, they came up with a strategy to defeat their enemy.

Ajay went first, swinging his hatchets at his target but he was too slow. The Geode-Stone humanoid easily side-stepped his attack. Saivik fired an electric pulse to follow up but the enemy jumped over his attempt. Little did the beast know, this was the opportunity they were looking for.

Myla charged in with her opponent in mid-air. She did a cartwheel before throwing a kick with her dominant leg. She thought she had a clear strike but when she got closer, the glare that was on the visor of the beast disappeared. Myla could see the face of the humanoid.

"Amrita?" She stopped her kick in mid-stride.

"Myla watch out!" Saivik shouted.

As she was lost in thought, her enemy was about to land a counterpunch. Ajay jumped in to grab Myla, saving her from a painful hit but in doing so, their enemy reoriented the attack and delivered two quick jabs, one to Ajay and the other to Myla.

Saivik saw both his allies down, so he jumped in against the speedster to stall for time. As they were battling, Ajay and Myla slowly pulled themselves up.

"Myla, what's wrong? You had that thing beat but you stopped!"

"Ajay, that thing is someone from our class."

"Who?"

"Amrita." When Ajay heard the name, his thoughts went back to the photo he saw in the book. Small memories of their time as classmates were returning to his mind.

"What are we going to do?"

"I... I don't know..."

The large group continued to follow Barmaan further into the Polluted Wilds and they could hear the wail from afar. Most of them were able to ignore the sound but Sarmaan could not. Instead of staying focused like everyone else, he felt something pulling him toward the wailing sound. He ran off, leaving the group confused.

"Sarmaan get back here! Stupid monkey dragged me all the way here and now runs away!" Shouted Ashima in outrage.

"You all go on ahead!" I will make sure nothing happens to him." Max assured everyone as he went after the runaway monkey.

"Okay everyone, let's follow Barmaan again and..." As Willyham was trying to refocus everyone, a barrage of shards was headed in his direction. Luckily, Harshitha sensed the attack in time and froze the attack with an ice wall spell.

The beast that launched the attack, revealed itself as the humanoid with long crystallized hair. Aria recognized their foe but before she could volunteer for the battle, Harshitha told her to press on as she requested to have Netanya and Ashima stay and fight instead.

"What?! Why them?!" Aria was furious.

"Yeah! Why me?!" Ashima was nervous as she didn't want to fight.

Harshitha explained to Aria that she had a feeling there would be tougher foes. She felt it made the most sense to keep Aria, Dante, and Arnav for those battles ahead. Aria was impressed by her foresight and because she was satisfied with her explanation, she left with Willyham, Arnav, Dante and Barmaan.

The humanoid enemy raised its hair in anticipation for the battle against the three heroines from Zenith. Seeing none of them making the first move, the beast rapidly fired shards from its hair toward the three targets.

Netanya cast a bubble shield over them and negated the attack. When the barrage was over, Harshitha cast an ice wave for Ashima to hop on. She guides the wave right at the beast, allowing Ashima to swing her hammer at melee range.

Their first attempt caught the enemy off-guard as the beast sustained damage to the abdomen area. However, the humanoid shook off the hit and shot out its shards in retaliation.

Again, Netanya shielded them and Ashima went for another full swing with her Geode-stone maul. The hammer made contact with their foe but this time, she used her hardened Geode-stone hair to create a cocoon for herself. It was tough enough to stop the maul's attack without gaining a scratch.

Ashima couldn't believe how tough the hair was so she repeatedly struck the cocoon in hopes of breaking through. The more she attacked, the more it changed colour. Ashima wasn't paying attention but Harshitha and Netanya both realized something wasn't adding up. When they saw the crystal cocoon turn full red, they warned Ashima to get out.

Unfortunately, Ashima was in mid-swing and when she struck the cocoon for the last time, it erupted with an explosion of energy. Ashima was caught in the blast but Harshitha and Netanya both cast their wind magic to soften Ashima's impact against the ground. They had safely placed Ashima on the ground and they turned to face their opponent. However, the enemy that they were about to face looked slightly different as it emerged out of the cocoon. In particular, they could see the face of the opponent they were battling.

"That's..." Harshitha started but Netanya finished. "Sissi..."

"Doom..." She echoed.

Harshitha braced herself for a tough battle. She asked to see if Netanya was ready but suddenly her ally dropped to the ground gasping for air. Harshitha was concerned as she wasn't sure what was happening until she looked around where they were standing. The cocoon explosion scattered debris from the forest, including tree nuts, one of Netanya's deadly allergies.

Absolute Nonsense

At the other battle, Sahil, Jacob, and Devan were all lying on their stomach struggling to get up. The giant Geode-stone beast was far stronger than they had anticipated. It also didn't help that Jacob and Sahil were still tired from their earlier battle.

Devan was the first to get up but when he asked the other two if they had any energy to fight, they were completely gassed out. He was left alone to face the giant beast along with all the other Geode-Mutants slowly creeping their way towards him.

He thought it was over until an arrow flew in and hit one of the mindless mutants. Then a few more arrows struck more of them and their attention was diverted to the archer who attacked them, Max.

Slowly, they moved to Max but Sarmaan came slamming into the fray in his gorilla form. He picked up one of the mutants and swung it at the other, knocking multiple enemies out at once.

After clearing a path, Sarmaan made his way to Devan and handed him a Geode-stone. When Devan received the gift, he had a rush of memories return. It was a time in Zenith when he, Jacob and Sarmaan (in human form) caused mischief among the public streets.

The swarm of mutants continued their march. Max couldn't fire his arrows quick enough and even Sarmaan was becoming overwhelmed by their sheer numbers. It seemed their rescue efforts were in vain until Devan jumped in front of them. Something about him was different from before.

"Now I remember. TEAM ABSOLUTE NONSENSE, ASSEMBLE!"

Upon his announcement, Jacob and Sarmaan had a resurgence of energy. The trio of Jacob, Devan and Sarmaan all did some strange dance moves before striking their unique hero pose. Sahil and Max looked at each other with the feeling of embarrassment and then looked away.

The lesser mutants were creating a wall to protect their leader. Sarmaan was up first, and the Geode-stone on his body began to glow, granting him extra power. The gorilla pounded the ground with both his fist and a rock wave appeared and wiped out almost a third of the mutant wall.

With a much weaker defence to break through, Devan put the Geode-stone he was given into the chest component of his suit. He felt a surge of power and he blitzed through the wall of Geode-Mutants, knocking the ones in his way.

He stopped right in front of the giant beast who towered over him. Devan provoked the beast to use his loud wail again. It was about to open its mouth but a bolt of lightning struck it on the shoulder. The plan was for Jacob to strike the beast right in the mouth but he had missed the intended target. That was their chance to end the battle but now the other minions were reforming the wall and Devan was about to get pummeled by the beast.

However, a rock hit the giant creature on the side of its forehead. Sahil managed to muster up his last ounce of strength to slapshot some rocks to distract their foe.

Max was running towards Jacob as he had an idea but there were many mutants blocking the way. Seeing Max's predicament, Sarmaan crashed in to create a clear path for Max. The former enforcer ran through the opening that Sarmaan temporarily created for him. After Max made it through, Sarmaan was swarmed and dogpiled by the army of mutants.

Thanks to Sarmaan's efforts, Max made it to Jacob and he asked him for his spear. Jacob was reluctant to give it but then he saw Devan barely surviving against the beast. Sahil could no longer help Devan as he too was overpowered by the enemy forces.

Seeing the dire situation they were in, Jacob handed his weapon over, putting all his faith in Max's plan. With the swarm of enemies approaching the remaining two fighters, Max took the spear and loaded it on his bow.

The beast had Devan trapped and he was about to unleash his deadly wail. As it was about to open its mouth, he noticed Jacob's spear headed its way so it moved its head over and the spear missed its target.

Max and Jacob were in absolute shock. Their gamble had failed and now the beast was about to direct its wail against them. It opened its mouth but right when it did, the spear was driven onto its tongue. Devan had caught the spear in mid-air after the miss without the beast noticing.

The creature attempted to shake the spear out of its mouth but a surge of electricity flowed from the weapon and into the tongue of the monster. The shock was dispersed through its entire body, causing a massive explosion which took out all the other Geode-Mutants.

Jacob, Sahil, Sarmaan, Max and Devan had survived but they were completely worn out. They were hoping that the battle was finally over but with the area still filled with smoke, they heard a sound and saw a shadow emerge.

"You have got to be kidding me!" Jacob said in disbelief.

"Anyone got anything left?" Devan asked.

"Guess this is the end of the road. It was nice knowing..." Sahil was interrupted.

"Wait!" Max called out and he slowly approached the silhouette. Everyone thought he was crazy but when Max got close enough to the figure, it suddenly fell through the smoke. The Geode-Mutant Beast was no more and instead, it was a small human man. Max caught him and when he saw the face, he instantly recognized him. It was one of their classmates from their time in Zenith, and a good friend of Max, 'Dylan!'

It Takes Two

Saivik and Ajay were breathing heavily as they had been battling the speedy Geode-Mutant with all their effort. In contrast, their opponent had barely broken a sweat and to make matters worse, Myla was not prepared mentally to face her opponent.

"Myla snap out of it! We need your help!" Ajay called out with urgency.

"I know but..."

Sensing her weakness, the speedster appeared in front of Myla but Saivik managed to intercept and block the attack. Saivik then pushed his opponent back a few feet so he could speak with Myla.

"Listen, if you aren't going to fight, then step aside. You are only hindering us right now."

"I..."

"So what's it going to be?" Saivik wanted a clear answer.

"Come on Myla, you can make the right choice." Ajay encouraged.

Their enemy who had been pushed back, grew furious. The Geode-Mutant channelled its energy and began circling the three fighters at high speed. It was so fast, it created a tornado that pulled them in.

Ajay dug both his hatchets against the ground and he held on tight. Saivik was able to drive the end of his electrical staff to the ground to prevent him from getting pulled away. But Myla didn't have anything to hang onto so she was taken away by the tornado which carried her in the air, flinging her to a different location.

"Myla!"

"Ajay focus."

"But Myla, she's..."

Saivik grabbed him by the shoulders and explained that if he wanted to help Myla, they had to first defeat the enemy that stood in their way. From that point onward, Ajay changed his attitude and prepared himself to fight. With his focus reestablished, Saivik told Ajay the plan of attack.

Ajay swung his hatchets at their foe who dodged his attack with ease. Despite the result, Ajay kept applying pressure even though it was the same result every time. He pushed the speedster back by a little but he could never land a hit.

Finally, their enemy got tired of dodging, so it retaliated with three quick consecutive jabs, knocking Ajay on his back. The creature had full confidence in its victory and Saivik thought his enemy had let its guard down. He jumped out and attempted to fire an electrical pulse from his gadget, but the mutant slipped past the attack.

The speedster reappeared in front of Saivik and repeatedly slapped him with its palm at high speed. Saivik was heavily beaten and dropped near a pond where he lay unconscious. The Geode-Mutant then turned around and moved towards Ajay.

With him lying on his back, the beast saw Ajay as no threat. It had its guard down and this was where Ajay capitalized by going for the enemy's legs, knocking it down. The speedster fell into the pond and was picking itself up. It was looking to get back at Ajay but then it noticed that Saivik was now up and standing at the pond with his electrical staff. That was when it realized that Saivik had this planned from the start.

He drove his weapon into the pond and once it made contact with the water, even the humanoid speedster couldn't outrun electricity. The high voltage was delivered through its entire body and the enemy collapsed into the water.

Both Ajay and Saivik were lying on the floor and they could relax for a bit after the effort they exerted. They laughed at the irony that not too long ago, Saivik was hunting Ajay down as a fugitive. Now, they fought alongside one another and some of their memories from years ago, returned.

Ajay was so lost in his mind that he wasn't aware that his enemy was now standing behind him. Thankfully, Saivik reacted by pushing Ajay to safety but for his action, the speedster struck Saivik in the liver.

Finally, Ajay snapped out of his trance and when he returned to reality, he saw Saivik lying unconscious after saving him. He couldn't forgive himself, thinking Saivik's current situation was all his fault.

Overwhelmed with emotions, Ajay fell to his knees. His opponent slowly walked up to him, thinking he was finished, but that was not the case. Ajay had been hiding his power because he refused to let anyone see the darker side of him. But with no one else around, he could freely use his technique. Both his hatchets and the Geode-stone he had began to flow with energy. His opponent didn't think it was possible but its eyes were not deceived. Ajay, a sapphire-ranked student could use Geode-breaker.

His two hatchets combined into one giant axe and his eyes were glowing. When he lifted his new weapon, a tremendous upward force could be felt by his enemy. It was so powerful, that it couldn't move, nullifying its greatest asset, its speed.

Without hesitation, Ajay swung his ultimate weapon and the Geode-Mutant took a critical hit. The armor on the creature was disappearing and what remained was a girl whom Ajay recognized as memories began appearing in his mind again. It was his classmate from their time in Diamondvale, Amrita.

She gently fell to the ground, lying near Saivik. Seeing them both safe, Ajay's Geode-breaker disappeared but he had exhausted too much energy. His fatigue caught up to him so he fell asleep and joined Saivik and Amrita on the ground.

Unlikely Encounter

After being flung into an unfamiliar part of the Polluted Wilds, Myla woke up. The first thing she saw was a lion near her face. She was startled initially but she remembered this lion was the same one she encountered not too long ago. She thanked the lion for his efforts but she also noticed a girl covering herself with a hood.

"Did you help rescue me too?"

"Not really, Leo over here did most of the work. I just made sure you didn't fall off his back."

Myla was taken back by her aloofness. She didn't have a positive impression of her until she noticed some drinking water was placed near where she woke up, and some of her wounds had been taped up. There was no way the lion did that for her, it had to be Keira.

"Thank you for helping me!"

Keira was surprised. She didn't think Myla would notice. "It was nothing." She pretended not to care.

After rehydrating herself with the water, she began heading out on her own.

"And where do you think you are going? Don't tell me you are planning on fighting those ugly things out there."

"Okay, I won't tell you then."

"Ugh!" She stomps on the ground in frustration.

Myla was perplexed. She wasn't sure what she did to make Keira so angry.

"You are all stubborn and crazy! You are not fully healed and yet you are recklessly going to fight again? Don't you realize how dangerous it is? Don't you care about your own life?"

Myla took a deep breath, hoping the right words would appear to her. "You are right, it's very dangerous and I'm not in prime fighting condition."

"Then why? It doesn't make any sense!"

"I know, but my friends are risking their lives and putting in all they got. I can't turn away from that."

As Myla was walking away, Keira reminisced about three people in her life. She remembered how courageous they were. How they would risk their lives to help others in need. These were memories Keira kept repressed because she thought they would be too painful to remember. However, seeing Myla exhibit similar traits as the people in her memories made her realize that it didn't have to be painful.

"Hey!" Myla stopped when she heard Keira call out. She caught up to Myla. "I'm tagging along."

"Are you sure? It's going to be quite dangerous out there." Myla joked.

"Ha, very funny. You don't have a choice, you need me."

"As if! Why would I need you?"

"Well for starters, you are going the wrong way."

"Oh, I knew that."

Keira smacked her forehead unimpressed, before calling for Leo. They all gathered together and Keira guided them to where they needed to go.

Triple Cast

Deep within the Polluted Wilds was a hidden laboratory filled with test subjects and vials of extracted Geode-stones. The lone scientist continued to go about his work when someone entered his lab.

"Headmaster Volice, have you brought me a new test subject?"

"No more test subjects."

"But sir, we agreed..."

"Plans have changed and time is of the essence. You will perform the procedure now." He demanded.

"None of the current test subjects will be able to handle the operation. They will all..." Before he could finish his sentence, Volice grabbed him by the throat.

"I guess you will have to do, Doctor Vihaan!"

He was prepared to use the scientist to move forward with the operation but stopping him was someone who had broken through the door. Without any concern, Volice turned to see who had entered.

"Always so punctual aren't you?" Rice didn't reply. "You are too late! This procedure is happening and you can't stop me!"

Volice sounded confident until Rice suddenly appeared in front of him. Volice was caught off-guard for a moment and he reacted but throwing a punch that clash against his opponent's fist. The impact of their attacks sent Vihaan into the air. Rice leaped and caught the scientist who was trying to gather his breath after such a collision.

Volice still had the look of determination but he was masking his fear. Rice was a much greater threat now as opposed to their encounter from years ago. He was readying himself for a difficult battle but Rice put down the scientist and signaled to Volice that he had no intention of fighting.

"Then why are you here?"

"I heard you need a test subject."

"And what if I do?

"I'm here to volunteer for that role."

H arshitha was breathing heavily as she was the only one capable of battling. Not only was her opponent tough, but she had other concerns. She had to be cautious with her spells as any strong iterations could cause collateral damage and harm Ashima who was lying on the floor. To compound her problems, she had to defeat her opponent quickly or Netanya's reaction would turn fatal.

In contrast, her opponent wasn't held back by any concerns. It raised its hair and launched projectile spikes at Ashima. Harshitha quickly cast an ice shield and jumped in front to block the attack. She successfully prevented Ashima from getting hit.

However, the Geode-Mutant's hair began to grow longer. It then strengthened it's hair and started to use them like whips that constantly lashed against Harshitha's ice shield. The attacks were slowly breaking off the ice and Harshitha didn't have a choice. She stayed there taking every hit to protect Ashima.

When the humanoid beast halted its assault, she found Harshitha still standing with cuts all over her arms and legs. "Is that all you got?"

The beast reacted by sending one of its hair at Harshitha but a bubble shield appeared and blocked the attack. Netanya managed to pick up her wand and cast the spell to help her friend. However, her allergic reaction returned, forcing her to drop her wand. Then, the enemy attacked by whipping her.

"Netanya!"

After seeing her friend severely injured, Harshitha recklessly charged at her opponent without thinking. As she did, Ashima's eyes were slowly opening and she saw the horrific sight of her ally taking a devastating hit from the beast.

The creature slowly walked away as Harshitha was lying down on the ground. It was then that memories of their times in Zenith resurfaced in their minds. The three girls were close friends who would studied together and annoyed their teachers instead of roaming around the campus.

As they remembered, Ashima reached out her hand to Harshitha even though they were too far apart to make contact. Harshitha could see her friend trying to help her but her injuries were too much, forcing her to close her eyes. Ashima could only watch as her friend was lying motionless on the ground.

Ashima was trying to keep it together by looking away. Unfortunately, her attention was now diverted to Netanya whose condition was now critical. It was too much for Ashima to take in as she covered her head and began to weep.

The beast felt a hint of sympathy for Ashima. It slowly guided its crystalized hair to encircle around Ashima and when it had fully wrapped around, it was ready to end the pain. However, when the creature exerted pressure, Ashima's hammer unleashed a pulse that repelled the hair back.

Ashima then picked up her weapon with both hands and then she smashed the ground with all her strength. The creature reacted by bracing herself, anticipating a massive shockwave but after a wave of light passed her, nothing happened.

The creature was disappointed by Ashima's attack, thinking it was all smoke and mirrors. It lashed its hair at the doctor but a bubble forcefield appeared and deflected all the hair wildly away. It looked back to find Netanya had somehow made a full recovery.

It was confused but wasn't concerned until it felt a blast of flame striking it from the blind side. Harshitha had landed a clean hit and now the creature was worried. It finally understood that Ashima's earlier attack wasn't meant to harm anyone. Instead, it was a healing wave disguised as a devastating attack.

The beast attempted to regain its composure by extending its hair but this time, it felt some resistance. It looked at its hair and saw that it had all been tangled. Netanya's last bubble shield spell forced the hair to bounce off randomly and tangle amongst each other. Now the creature's hair was in many knots.

With its greatest weapon nullified, it shivered in fear as Harshitha unleashed her Geode-Breaker. For a brief moment, she was given an immense amount of energy that was stored in her source. With all this energy, it gave her the ability to cast one of the most destructive spells known to all mages.

Feeling its life threatened, the beast attempted to flee but Ashima slammed the ground with her hammer and radiant chains burst from below to restrain their foe.

Channelling a majority of the energy stored in her orb, Harshitha had her palm opened up to the sky. Clouds began to form and raining down from the sky were meteors infused with her magical energy. Although this spell was powerful it came with huge drawbacks, one being that Harshitha couldn't control where all the meteors would land.

Many would strike around the vicinity of her enemy, who was bound to the ground by Ashima, but the rest were a coin toss. Some of them were heading straight for Harshitha and Ashima. Knowing the risks, Harshitha accepted it but she also put an immense amount of trust in her teammates. Casting a bubble forcefield over the three of them was Netanya.

When the barrage of meteors subsided, Netanya released the forcefield. Harshitha and Ashima were both unharmed. The only question left was if their enemy had survived. Together, they walked towards the field of meteorites and they found a body lying there. The Geode-Mutant was nowhere to be detected. In its place was one of their classmates from years ago, Sissi.

Deceit

After what seemed like an eternity traversing the Polluted Wilds, Barmaan led the small crew to a laboratory hidden deep within the forest. Willyham was excited to see something other than just trees but everyone else was worried about what was within the building.

As they approached the entrance, they saw a familiar face that gave them peace of mind.

"Rice!" Dante shouted as the man stood there without a reply.

"Where is Vihaan and Master Volice? Asked Arnav.

"Inside."

"Everyone is giving it their all. Let's defeat that dumb headmaster and get Vihaan out of here!" Aria announced.

"Everyone follow Barmaan!" Willyham exclaimed.

Barmaan took one step forward but his instinct sensed an ominous presence heading towards them. The lizard lept in front of the person who was about to be struck. Barmaan took a hit that was meant for Willyham. However, the force of the attack was so great that Barmaan ended up crashing into Willyham and they were both sent slamming into a tree. They lay on the ground temporarily unresponsive.

Dante, Arnav and Aria were in shock as to what happened because the one who landed the attack wasn't someone they had expected to be their enemy.

"I will be your opponent," Rice informed them as he shook his fist after landing the punch.

In another area of the Polluted Wilds, Keira, Myla and Leo continued walking.

"Leo, are we there yet?" Keira complained but Leo returned with a quiet grumble.

"How about now?" She asked after ten seconds.

"Seriously? How do you deal with this?" Myla asked the lion.

"Hey, who are you complaining about?"

"Me? Complaining!? Do you hear yourself? You have done nothing but ask that annoying 'are we there yet' question for hours!"

"Listen Drama Queen, we haven't been walking for an hour and I'm sick of your attitude!"

"DRAMA QUEEN?! Why you little..."

The two were about to throw punches at each other. Leo was rolling his eyes in response to their immaturity but suddenly he stopped, and both Keira and Myla bumped into his back.

"Oww... Leo, what's the deal? That..." Keira held out her hand to tell Myla to be quiet. Without their arguing they could all sense the ground rumbling.

Bursting out of the ground were the mindless Geode-Mutants. The three of them were trying to find their balance from all the shaking but once they regained their footing, they looked on and saw the countless number of enemies before them.

Leo initiated as he jumped into the fray by himself and when Myla saw him, she was ready to follow but Keira stopped her.

"What are you doing? We can't just leave him alone."

"I know." Keira pointed to the direction for Myla to go. "I'll stay behind, you go on and help your friends."

"But..."

"There's no time to turn this into a drama, now go!"

Myla was about to leave but she had one last thing to say to Keira. "Thank you."

Keira tried to hide it but a smile broke on her face. Myla turned away and ran while Keira jumped into battle to support Leo against the multitudes of Geode-Mutants.

Myla continued moving forward because she knew that the fighting would not end until they stopped Volice. Eventually, the laboratory was in Myla's line of sight. She was ready to make the final stretch to her destination until she saw someone struggling to stand up.

She rushed towards the person in need and after asking to see his condition, the man looked up and Myla immediately recognized him.

"Vihaan! You are alive!"

"I'm glad to see you too." Vihaan had something urgent to say but his body was growing weaker as every second passed.

"Take it easy, whatever you have to tell me can wait. We need to get you medical attention first."

"There is no time! As we speak Dante, Aria, and Arnav are battling against Rice."

"What?!" Myla was conflicted. She couldn't accept that their former teacher was their enemy. However, if what Vihaan said was true, Myla couldn't fathom the amount of danger her friends were in. She was about to rush to their rescue but Vihaan stood in her way.

"Vihaan, I have to help them! Get out of my way!"

"No, they aren't the ones who need your help, but someone else does."

"Who are you talking about?"

"Let me explain..."

No Holding Back

The clouds in the air were moving quickly as they were beginning to cover the sun. It seemed it would inevitably rain but for the time being, the ground remained dry. However, down on the battlefield, Aria, Dante, and Arnav were all already sweating.

The fight had barely begun but they found themselves struggling against their foe. Even with their combined efforts, they knew this was going to be a difficult struggle. As the three continued to breathe heavily, Rice took a couple of steps forward.

"Are you three really students of mine? I thought you were all much stronger."

Dante and Arnav weren't bothered by the insult but something within Aria lit up. She dashed passed her friends and engaged the heavily favoured opponent all by herself.

When Rice saw that Aria had separated from the two boys, his plan was set into motion. Dante noticed what Rice was planning so he tried to warn Aria but it was too late. With Aria a couple meters away from striking, Rice threw down a Geode-stone beneath her feet. From the Geode-stone, a giant mist appeared and encircled a large portion of the battlefield. Aria and Rice were caught inside while Dante and Arnav remained outside.

Sensing Aria was in danger, they ran to the mist hoping to find their friend but when they attempted to enter from one side, they immediately fell out on the other side of the forest. No matter how hard they tried, they couldn't get in to help Aria.

Dante's scanners couldn't identify a solution to their problem. While Arnav's sword swing couldn't cut into the mist. It seemed there was no physical barrier to break but they wouldn't quit. The two kept working on a solution.

Inside, Aria saw nothing but open space surrounded by the mist. When she tried to run through the mist she would end up on the other side of the arena. She was worried initially that she was trapped inside alone until she noticed that her enemy was in front of her. She was glad that she was the one fighting Rice and not Dante or Arnav.

Her opponent suddenly appeared within range to strike her with a right cross. At the last second, Aria blocked the attack with her forearms. She was pushed back towards the edge of the arena and when her body made contact with the mist, her entire body went through.

Just like before, she teleported to the other side of the battlefield. As she was still sliding back from the momentum, her back was now facing her enemy. Aria could sense she was vulnerable from behind. With haste, she turned around to reduce the impact by taking Rice's attack to the shoulder.

In total, she had only taken two hits but she could feel her arms shaking. The power behind the two punches was far stronger than she had anticipated. Although this would cause most to coward in fear, Aria was strangely energized by this feeling. The thrill of battle got her thinking on her feet and after getting some air into her brain, she figured out a plan of attack.

She dashed at Rice directly, only to be sent back by his counter. She was thrown with such force, that she fell through the mist again and reappeared on the other side. Anticipating this would happen, Aria had her body turned around preemptively and she used that momentum she gained to direct a punch right at Rice.

He managed to block Aria's fist with his left arm, sending Aria back to the mist but again she reappeared on the opposite side and attacked Rice from a different angle. Aria would keep using the special properties of the misty arena to keep pace with her opponent's power.

Both fighters should have been getting slower and more fatigued as the battle drew on, but that was not the case. Instead, the two fighters seemed more energized with each exchange as their focus was completely locked in.

Although Rice expected Aria to figure out how the effects of the misty arena worked, he was amazed by how quickly she came to that conclusion. He was proud and in that moment, memories of his time in Zenith appeared in his mind. What he saw were all the times he helped train Aria's classmates. The greatest joy he felt was seeing them improve little by little each day.

As Rice was reminiscing, Aria was still dialled in the fight. She could sense her opponent's focus slipping but more importantly, she believed she had a chance to win. Aria saw an opening to land a right hook at the rib area and she knew she had to take the chance.

When her punch was about an inch away, a sudden light flashed before her eyes. At that moment, the memories of her entire life ran through her mind. First, the memories of her times with her family, then her friends at Diamondvale, and finally her times at the Amazon Borderlands.

After feeling the experience of having her life flash before her eyes, she was about to be engulfed by a radiant light. However, the light suddenly shattered and she saw Rice standing in her mind.

"You have grown so strong in such a short time. If you only had another year or so, the result of our battle could have ended very differently. I'm sorry I had to cut our battle short, but time is of the essence. Take care of everyone. Goodbye." And he disappeared from her mind.

Arnav continued swinging his sword against the misty barrier but nothing changed. Dante's computer had been searching for a solution and still couldn't find any. They were beginning to grow anxious waiting when they noticed the barrier of the mist was shrinking.

They could see a silhouette of a person standing who appeared to be Aria's height. When the mist fully dissipated, they saw Aria's body standing but her eyes were closed and slowly she began to faint. Thankfully, someone caught her and placed her down gently to the ground, Rice.

Dante and Arnav looked on in dismay as they saw their friend defeated. They could handle Aria being unable to beat Rice in a battle, but what caused them concern was the condition Aria was in. She seemed, lifeless.

"What did you do to her?" The cyborg was seething with anger but his opponent continued to stand still with his arms crossed.

Dante's sensors were going off the charts. It constantly kept alerting him that his foe was too high of a threat level and that he should disengage immediately but he refused to listen. He was about to switch into battle mode but Arnav intervened. He tried to calm Dante down but Rice provoked the cyborg by turning his back on them. In that instance, Dante's anger took over and he ignored all warnings his systems were giving him.

His rocket boosters activated, leaving Arnav in his dust as he charged head-on against Rice. Arnav knew their chances of winning were slim but at this point, there was no use holding back. He joined Dante in the fray.

Amid his advance, Dante had his right arm transformed into a cannon. When he was in point-blank range, he was ready to unleash it at full power. Rice reacted by swatting the cyborg's arm, switching the new target of the cannon to Arnav. Dante tried to pull his cannon back but it was too late, his cannon unleashed a pulse wave that was about to hit Arnav directly. Thankfully, Arnav held out his shield which absorbed the attack.

Dante was relieved to see his friend survive his attack without a scratch. But right as they let their guard down, Rice appeared behind Arnav grabbing one of his forearms, forcing him to drop his shield. Seeing his comrade in pain, Dante was about to activate his thrusters to help Arnav.

Rice sensed what Dante was about to do. He stomped on Arnav's shield, flipping it up to a level where he could grab it with his right hand. He then threw the shield and it clashed against one of Dante's thrusters, disrupting it entirely. With only one thruster operational, Dante began flying around uncontrollably.

Thinking Rice had his attention diverted, Arnav swung his sword but his enemy slipped under it. He then picked up Arnav and threw him into the air. It was so well timed, that when Arnav was about to drop, Dante slammed into him and together they came crashing down.

The two warriors picked themselves up, breathing heavily. They knew they were outclassed but they refused to give in. Arnav held his sword with shaking hands while Dante's systems continued to warn him. "Systems damage, repairs needed. Further combat is not advised." They ignored it all and stood ready to continue the fight.

"Stop holding back." Arnav was confused as to what Rice was referring to. Dante told Arnav not to listen as he figured Rice was trying to mess with their minds.

"You both are far stronger than this. Stop hiding your power."

Arnav looked at his Geode-Stone for a moment and all he could remember was when he had lost control of that power. Seeing his friend conflicted, Dante jumped in.

"Stop it! I don't have any hidden power! Besides, how would you know?"

"Did you forget? I helped train you." Dante fell silent as Rice continued. "Not just you, every one of your classmates I have taught. I know what you are all capable of. Now, reveal your power. No holding back!"

Dante tried but his system kept telling him that he was at his limit. "I can't!"

Rice looked at the two students. Arnav was full of doubt while Dante was frustrated. He walked over to where Aria was lying down before speaking again.

"See your friend here? This will happen to all your classmates."

He caught both Arnav and Dante's attention and he also filled them with despair.

"Why! Why are you doing this??! Dante cried out but the man refused to answer. He gave them ten seconds to respond to his threat but nothing changed.

"It appears I was wrong. You both have reached your limit." He turned his back towards them.

"Wait, where are you going?!" Arnav asked with fear.

"I'm a man of my word. Since you couldn't show me any reasons to continue our battle, I will have to go after your classmates." He looked around and saw Willyham and Barmaan still unconscious. He announced to Arnav and Dante that those would be his first targets.

Arnav fell to his knees holding the Geode-stone in his hand. He kept staring at the stone and thinking what if he lost control again? He didn't want to hurt any of his friends.

Dante's system continued to display 'limit reached.' Nothing changed and Rice was tired of waiting. He appeared before Willyham and Barmaan ready to grab a hold of them. However, before he could do so, he sensed two masses of energies storming his way.

First, he avoided a swift sword swing that forced him to jump away from Willyham and Barmaan. Then he had to face a barrage of missiles which he had to strategically maneuver through. After dodging those attacks, he found himself facing two replenished fighters, Arnav who activated his Geode-breaker and Dante whose screen had shattered so he could no longer see the words 'limit reached.'

Fatal Strike

"**C**ome on Vihaan, we have to hurry!"

Myla was urging the scientist to pick up the pace. He had told everything to Myla and they needed to stop what was about to transpire.

"Hold on a minute."

"How could you be out of breath already?"

"Don't know if you've noticed but I've been cooped up in a lab for a couple of years. I no longer have the stamina I once had."

"Ugh, Vihaan this is no time to be..."

In the middle of her sentence, they felt the ground shake momentarily and they also saw a huge flash of light.

"What is happening?!" Myla asked in confusion.

"Oh no... Arnav and Dante... We have to go now!"

Vihaan had a sudden burst of speed as he passed Myla. "Hey! Wait for me!"

There was another sparring exchange between the three fighters. Although Arnav and Dante were sweating like before, they could sense something off about their opponent. His movement seemed slower and more predictable. They figured if they fought on a little longer, they would have a chance.

On the other side, Rice was concealing something from the two fighters. Something was hindering his strength but he ignored it and focused on the battle at hand.

Arnav and Dante both charged from the front hoping to overpower their foe. Rice responded by stomping his foot on the ground and throwing a punch. The force behind the attack sent Dante flying into the air but Arnav held on by driving his sword to the ground.

Once the attack wore off, Arnav threw his shield at Rice, who easily slipped through. He then appeared close to Arnav, pressuring his former student with a combination of jabs to prevent him from swinging his sword offensively.

When Rice saw an opening, he threw a cross right at Arnav's chest but he managed to block with his sword. Arnav was pushed back quite the distance and Rice was about to strike again until he sensed Dante hovering in the air behind him. The cyborg had Arnav's shield and he threw it in Rice's direction.

It should have been a routine dodge for Rice but he had a slight cough, so the shield nicked a piece of his clothing. Whatever he was hiding, was starting to take effect on the surface.

Arnav had successfully claimed his shield thanks to Dante's effort. He then held it in front and advanced towards his opponent. The shield made contact with Rice's hands and that began a pushing match between the two combatants. Initially, their strength seemed equal but over time, Arnav's strength was starting to give out. Rice was pushing back with Arnav about to fall on his knees. He was about to be crushed until Dante charged in from Rice's blindside with his arm transformed into a bladed weapon.

Rice's attention was now directed at Dante which allowed Arnav to get back on his feet and grip his sword properly. Now Rice was facing both his opponents who were planning to strike him simultaneously. He was ready to counter their attacks and when they clashed, the battle was over.

Aria who had been unconscious during the whole fight, suddenly woke up as if she had experienced a terrible nightmare. She had the feeling that someone she knew had passed away.

At about the same time, Vihaan and Myla had just appeared. Myla was glad to see Aria conscious but she wasn't prepared to witness what had happened near Dante and Arnav.

Rain

With the lesser Geode-Mutants dispersed and Dylan back to human form, Devan went to search for Sarmaan while Jacob stayed to see if he could help Sahil. Devan found Sarmaan lying on the ground, buried by some debris in his monkey form. He removed the stones in his way so he could retrieve the monkey to safety.

Meanwhile, Max put Dylan on his back and began to carry him. As he was returning to join the others, the rain began to pour down heavily on them.

They all looked up at the sky and somehow they all shared a similar feeling. Someone that they knew, was no longer physically in this world.

Elsewhere, Ajay and Saivik each put one of Amrita's arms over their shoulder. Together they carried their classmate to safety. It didn't take long before the sky was filled with grey clouds and rain poured down on them. They too felt the weight of losing someone they knew.

With Ashima's medical expertise, she managed to stabilize Sissi's condition. Harshitha was ready to carry her on her back when a massive downpour of rain appeared. Netanya put up her bubble forcefield to provide cover for everyone. Even though they couldn't feel the raindrops on their skin, they shared the feeling of losing someone they knew.

Keira and Leo were trapped in a corner against the endless mobs of Geode-Mutants. They thought they were goners until the rain began to pour down. The mindless mutants suddenly lost their will to fight. They slowly drifted away leaving Keira and Leo alone.

The little rogue was confused as to how they survived. She was about to celebrate how lucky they had gotten but when she turned around, she saw Leo sitting still and looking up to the rainy sky, knowing someone he had known was no longer around.

Willyham felt something trying to get his attention. He opened his eyes and saw Barmaan gently headbutting his shoulder. Finally, Willyham got up to rub his eyes and when he was done, he found Aria, Vihaan, Myla, Arnav, and Dante all standing in the monsoon.

He was glad to see everyone but he felt something was wrong. He approached them to ask what happened. Most of them couldn't find the words to speak but Dante spoke up.

"Let's move on, we still have Volice to take care of."

Willyham didn't speak any further but he felt anxious not knowing anything. As Arnav, Myla and Aria followed behind Dante's lead, Vihaan walked up beside Willyham and shared with him the event that took place not too long ago.

30 minutes earlier...

"Vihaan slow down! How in the world did you get so fast all of a sudden?"

Vihaan was running up the hill and Myla lagged behind. When he reached the top of the hill, he stopped, allowing Myla to catch up to him.

"Whew! You are fast for a scient..." She stopped mid-sentence as something on the battlefield caught her attention.

Dante and Arnav were about to strike at Rice from two directions. Rice was confident he could counter both their attacks. However, during their attack, Rice's body began acting up and he began coughing. For a moment, Rice was completely vulnerable.

Arnav and Dante could feel something wrong and they wanted to retract their attack but it was too late, they couldn't stop their momentum. Arnav's sword and Dante's blade pierced through Rice's body.

Arnav released his grip from the sword and Dante detached his blade from his arm. They immediately caught him before he could fall to the ground. "Heh, well done you two. You passed the test."

"No! That wasn't us! That doesn't count!" Arnav shouted.

"Why? Why did you have to change sides and betray us?!"

Before he had a chance to speak, Vihaan ran down the hill to defend Rice. "He didn't betray you guys! He..." Vihaan would have continued but Rice asked him to stop.

"When I first met you all as your teacher, I knew everyone in your class had great potential. You two were no exception, but you were both far too nice. For you to face the dangers ahead, you need to throw that part of you away."

That was when Dante pieced it together. He realized now that Rice pretended to be the enemy to draw out his and Arnav's powers. Arnav was about to speak but Rice's cough returned and it was worse than before. In addition to the coughing, the skin on his right arm was deteriorating.

"What's happening to him?" Arnav asked while Dante scanned through Rice's body to find that his condition was nearing fatal.

"This can't be possible, you are way stronger than this. Our attacks couldn't have caused this!" Dante was struggling to comprehend.

"It's from the experiment, isn't it? Your body couldn't handle it but you were hiding it this whole time." Vihaan spoke directly to Rice who replied with nothing but a smile.

Dante aggressively grabbed Vihaan by the collar of his lab coat. "What experiment? What did you do to him?!"

"Leave him alone Dante. I volunteered, it is not his fault." Dante let go of the scientist but he punched the ground in frustration. Right after, Myla rushed in unexpectedly and kicked Rice in the ribs.

"Myla what are you doing?! Can't you see what kind of condition he is in?" She ignored Vihaan.

"What kind of teacher puts their students through that level of emotional turmoil!" She was fuming yet at the same time, tears were dropping from her eyes.

"A lousy one." He still had a smile and his students couldn't believe how he could still be joking at a time like this. The infection was spreading and it was about to overtake him.

When Dante saw that his condition had gone from worse to fatal in a short duration, he was reminded of Aria. "We have to move fast, someone go get Aria, we have to get these two out of here now!" Dante urgently commanded but Rice interceded.

"Aria will be fine." He assured them as he held a vial with a concoction that only Vihaan knew about. It was a serum capable of keeping someone unconscious and making them seem lifeless. "The effects should be wearing off now."

"But that still leaves you. You need medical attention!" Arnav exclaimed.

"You are far stronger than this! Hang on, I will find a cure!" Vihaan declared.

When Rice heard those words from the scientist, it reminded him of a time when he was incapable of saving someone he knew. That was the day he decided to become stronger. In his final moments, he had one last message for them all. "Get strong, because if you are weak, you are of no help to anyone."

Dante, Arnav, and Vihaan stood still but Myla began shouting again. "Hey! Don't you dare leave us! You still need to say goodbye to every..." As she pulled on one of his arms, she felt his strength had left him and he was no longer breathing.

Together, Dante, Arnav, Vihaan, and Myla were silent. Aria, who was crawling her way towards everyone stopped a couple meters short when she saw what happened. That was when the dark clouds filled the sky and the torrential downpour began. Each drop of rain felt heavy and as they fell on their skin, they slowly regained memories of their time together in Zenith. Especially ones with their mean yet goofy teacher, Rice.

The Laboratory

Volice sat alone within the confines of the laboratory mulling over everything that had happened. He could feel that the presence of his greatest adversary was no longer around. This was not how he had imagined things to be but he had no time to be concerned with such matters as he sensed unwanted visitors near his territory.

The door creaked as it opened and entering were: Aria, Arnav, Vihaan, Myla, Dante, Willyham and Barmaan. Upon entering, they felt an aura of dread through the entire area. Even Vihaan who had been here for so long, never got used to such an atmosphere.

Once they fully entered the building, the door slammed shut behind them. Aria tried slamming into the door to push it open but to no avail. She resorted to punching the door but while she was pre-occupied doing so, a trapdoor activated beneath Willyham and Barmaan. Arnav stretched out to try to grab his arm but they had fallen out of reach. The trapdoor closed and suddenly their group had decreased by two.

"Everyone stay close to me, I'll help get us..." Vihaan was cut off as the lights went out. None of them could see anything so Dante activated his night vision and saw a switch.

"I think I found the switch for the lights, just give me a second." As Dante was moving, Vihaan could hear the cyborg's footsteps.

"Wait Dante don't, that switch is..." Vihaan's warning came too late as Dante pressed the switch. Suddenly, there was a scream before someone disappeared. Vihaan quickly made his way through the darkness, trusting his memory. He found the switch he was looking for and the lights had returned. The only problem was their party had once again shrunk. Myla, Arnav and Vihaan were the only ones remaining.

With their friends gone, they knew there was only one option and that was to press forward. Vihaan led the way, helping them avoid all the traps laid through the premises.

They kept walking through the area that seemed more like a haunted mansion than a lab. They came to a halt when Vihaan led them to an elevator. He pressed the button and they waited for the arrival of their ride.

That was the moment they let their guard down as something grabbed Arnav's leg. He reached for his sword but he got pulled out of sight. Right after Arnav's disappearance, the elevator door opened but Myla refused to get in as she wanted to go after Arnav.

Vihaan sensed something else headed in their direction. He pushed Myla into the elevator and she fell on her back. She was slow to get up and by the time she did, Vihaan had pressed the button to close the doors. She attempted to hold the doors open but it already closed on her. She slammed the elevator in frustration as Vihaan risked his life to get her closer to Volice.

The elevator descent felt like an eternity for Myla. She had all that time to herself and she couldn't wait for the doors to open so she could take out her anger on Volice. When the elevator hit the bottom floor, it stopped and the doors slid open.

Once she exited the elevator, she found herself in the laboratory. Everything on this level was what she expected to see in a mastermind's science facility. Large containment cells, science apparatus, and unknown chemicals everywhere.

After making it to the end of the lab, she found herself staring at the mastermind behind the creation of the Geode-Mutants, Headmaster of Diamondvale, Volice.

He greeted Myla with a warm welcome but she was not in the mood. "Vihaan told me everything." She replied.

"Oh, then you can see the nobility in my cause?"

You have to stop this now! What you're trying to accomplish isn't..."

Without any warning, Volice shouted, "Silenced!" Not only could she no longer speak, but her body was paralyzed. While she was restrained, Volice revealed how close he was to accomplishing his plans years ago. However, one teacher and a class of students delayed his work.

"Tch, of all the classes within Diamondvale, your group was the one I expected the least from. As a class, you were so dysfunctional and unable to work together. And yet, it was your class that discovered my plans and attempted to stop me.

Fortunately for me, you were all weak. In addition, the presence of your class hindered Rice from fighting at his full strength. None of you should have caused me any problems.

Especially you, since you weren't the strongest, fastest or smartest. Therefore, you should have posed no threat and yet out of your entire class, you became my biggest concern. Your positivity and tenacious attitude were contagious. Your teammates were able to keep fighting because of your energy.

The battle got drawn out longer than it should have and an explosion occurred within this very lab. Some of you escaped thanks to Rice while some became my test subjects. Then there were the ones back in Zenith, whose memories I had to alter.

My research with the Geode-stones was put to the test. Through years of hard work, I discovered how the crystals could have a profound impact on one's memory. With the Geode-stones being used everywhere on Zenith, to its waste being transferred down into the wasteland of Nadir, everyone's memory got altered. All except those who built an immunity to them."

Myla was sick and tired of hearing the old man ramble. She struggled to break free from the silent curse. Volice was not surprised to see Myla's refusal to quit but he was about to show her how futile her efforts were.

With the push of a button, six containment cells lit up. To Myla's dismay, each of them contained the following people: Dante, Arnav, Vihaan, Willyham, Barmaan, and Aria. A massive amount of their energy was being transferred into a Geode-stone. Volice then grabbed the stone and he was fed with all their powers. Myla looked on in despair as Volice could think of no better way to defeat his foe than with her own friends' powers.

As Myla stood still, Volice first used Arnav's shield charge and bashed Myla against a table. As she slowly pulled herself up, Volice's arm fired a pulse blast hitting Myla against a wall. She got up again and this time, Volice called on Aria's strength. He delivered Aria's signature combination attack, finishing with a cross punch at Myla's gut. After taking a hit from one of her closest friend's attacks, she was unable to get up.

Defiant Class

Seeing Myla unable to get back on her feet, VoIice moved towards her. He held out his fist and using the Geode-stone, he was about to summon Aria's power once more to conclude the fight.

Myla could hear Voice's footstep approaching but she thought it was all over. She saw the boots of the headmaster near her and she slowly looked up to face her enemy. However, upon doing so, she couldn't believe whose face she saw.

She thought she was hallucinating so she rubbed her eyes to make sure. With her vision clear, the face remained there. Somehow, she was able to see Rice but she had to be dreaming.

"Ha, you are about to lose to an old man. Are you really going to let this happen?"

His comment aggravated her so much that it revitalized her fighting spirit. "I'm going to kick that smirk right off your face!"

A burst of energy came to Myla and she did a flip kick right at the man's face. She thought she landed a clean kick on Rice but when she looked again, it was Voice who took the hit.

Voice was taken by surprise but he should have known better than to let his guard down. He regathered the energy needed to end the fight. Myla knew she had to dodge but her body was no longer listening. Her flip kick expended nearly all the energy she had and now, she had to accept her fate.

As Voice was about to land the finishing blow, a forcefield appeared before Myla. She looked to the side and saw Netanya casting the shield spell. Voice was baffled because he knew Netanya alone couldn't create a barrier strong enough to stop him. Taking a closer look, he saw Harshitha and Ashima assisting Netanya by empowering the forcefield.

Seeing the trio working together gave him concern, so he pressed a button in his lab and it opened a hidden door that released a wave of lesser Geode-Mutants. Free from their containment, they marched towards their enemies. However, their numbers would be greatly reduced as the rest of the class appeared to take on the mindless creatures.

Saivik and Sahil worked together by keeping their distance from the mob of Geode-Mutants. Saivik fired electrical pulses from his wrist and Sahil slapshot any debris he could find against the mutants.

Following up was Team Absolute Nonsense consisting of Jacob, Devan and Sarmaan. Jacob held his spear up high, Devan braced himself to charge against his foes, and Sarmaan transformed into his gorilla form. Together, they mauled through their enemies with loud and strange warcries. Devan tackled all the mutants, Sarmaan slammed them against one another and Jacob electrocuted them.

Then there were Amrita, Sissi, and Dylan. The three temporarily regained their Geode-Mutant forms but this time, they had full control over their powers. Sissi's hair shards easily took out a squad of the mutants. Amrita ran a full circle around another group, creating a tornado that blew them against the wall. Finally, Dylan let out the biggest wail he could muster and scared off the multitude of Geode Mutants.

Next, Ajay, Max, and Leo joined the battle. Ajay swung his hatchets rapidly, knocking aside any mutants in his path. Any targets that Ajay couldn't reach, Max picked off using his archery skills and Leo would slash away the rest with his lion claws.

With their combined efforts, they were able to repel the Geode-Mutants. However, Volice had witnessed enough. In his rage, he let out a bellow and anything caught within his aura was being suppressed against the ground by a heavy gravitational force. He had them in a similar situation years ago, but this time he was determined to end it.

With his focus on all the students before him, he didn't notice someone tampering with his computer system, which messed up the power in the entire room. As the lights began flashing, he turned around to find the one person he didn't account for, Keira.

Seeing the culprit who was disrupting his lab, he called forth Dante's cyborg arm and aimed his attack at the Keira. Myla warned her but Keira was too focused on making sure she completely dismantled the computer system within the lab. She chose to finish the job but Volice fired the pulse beam that was headed straight for her.

"No!" Myla cried but it wasn't Keira who took the hit. Jumping in front of her was Leo who blocked the beam and he fell to the ground, heavily injured.

Keira immediately yelled for him to get up but there was no response.

Volice showed no remorse and he was ready to strike at Keira again but smashing out of her containment cell was Aria who had awakened thanks to Keira's efforts. She jumped onto the next cell, breaking Dante free and then Arnav's.

Together, they combined their efforts of Dante's missile barrage, Arnav's sword slashes, and Aria's dash punches to clear out the remaining mutants. The only enemy left was Volice.

Volice was about to replenish his energy with the Geo-stone but when he looked at his hand, the crystal was missing. He looked around and found Keira with the Geo-stone in her possession. While Volice was distracted, she used her tape to steal the stone from him. All he had left to depend on was his remaining energy but it might be enough as Dante, Aria and Arnav were close to exhausting everything in the tank. The three engaged against the headmaster in hopes they had enough energy left.

Myla watched the battle taking place, and she knew their efforts wouldn't be enough to defeat Voice. She could finally get up as Voice's gravitational field was weakened since he was busy battling her comrades. Myla wanted to join the fight but her body wouldn't cooperate.

She thought she could only helplessly watch until Vihaan shouted a message to everyone. He told them to lend their energy to the fighters who were still standing. Those who had their Geode-stones, raised them and those who were in their Geode Mutant forms raised their hands to give away their remaining energy.

Arnav, Dante, and Aria were barely able to move. Voice thought he had them beaten but the energies from their classmates reached their bodies and were shared between them. Not only did they feel rejuvenated, but many of their memories also returned. All the good times, tough times, and most importantly, all the training and combat experience they had, all returned.

Voice's power had declined so much that his aura was no longer able to suppress anyone. Instead, he had to save all his energy into fighting the three enemies who stood before him.

Arnav took the lead by using his shield charge technique. Voice held his ground as he was able to prevent Arnav from overpowering him. The Headmaster was about to counter attack but he saw Dante jumping above Arnav, ready to launch his sonic cannon.

Right at that moment, Arnav gave an extra push to force Voice away from him, giving Dante a clear line of fire. His sonic cannon attack was directed at Voice and he had no choice but to brace himself for the attack. The headmaster managed to use some of his energy to block Dante's attack but it left him vulnerable to a blindside uppercut from Aria.

He took the uppercut but as she attempted to follow up with another punch, Voice grabbed her arm. He had Aria in his grasp, but kicking him in the liver was Myla. The impact caused him to let go of Aria and together, the two girls struck him simultaneously.

After his body was dragged against the ground from the last attack, Volice was slow to get up and he wasn't going to catch any breaks. As he looked up, he saw the four fighters approaching in different directions. They all got ready for one final strike but Volice concentrated his remaining energy to unleash a nova pulse around him that struck all four warriors and sent them back against the ground.

Volice was huffing for air after expending all that energy. Slowly, he regained his normal breathing and he began to smile, thinking he had finally won. But out of the debris, the four fighters rose again.

"Impossible!" was what he thought to himself initially until the dust behind the fighters cleared up and he saw what he was truly up against. Beyond Dante, Aria, Myla, and Arnav, he saw the entire class standing behind them and for a slight moment, a spirit that resembled their teacher appeared.

With his energy near depleted, he turned around hoping to escape but as he did, one person stood in his way. Waiting with a smile was Willyham who confidently told him there was nowhere left for him to run. Even though Volice was weakened, he had enough power to push Willyham aside. However, before he could lift his arm, he felt something biting on his leg, Barmaan.

"Ugh! Annoying little..." He shook off Barmaan but as Volice turned his focus back to Willyham, he had disappeared. It was all a distraction to buy enough time to prevent the headmaster from escaping.

Realizing his defeat was imminent, Volice turned to face his enemies. With the energy of all their classmates, Arnav attacked first with his sword shattering Volice's first layer of his aura shield. Dante followed up with his sonic pulse canon that demolished another layer. The third and final layer was smashed through by Aria's fist, leaving

Myla an opening to finish it off. She spun in the air three times before delivering the kick right at Volice's body.

Secrets Unveiled

Inside the headmaster's mind, he heard the voice of a little boy. It brought back memories of the bright smile the kid had and his spirit for life was unmatched. It was a sense of joy that he had not felt in a long time.

Returning his focus to reality, he saw the four fighters barely standing. He also saw the look on the entire class as they couldn't believe he was still standing. Voice took one step and immediately, everyone braced themselves for the worse. Contrary to what they were expecting, the headmaster moved a short distance to find a comfortable area to rest. When he located his desired spot, he sat down and spoke his mind.

He was remembering the happiest day of his life. It was a day he would never forget because it was the birth of his son. Despite his busy schedule as the head of the school, Voice always found time for his son, whether it was for dinner time or playtime. They developed a strong father-son bond over the years and his son had dreams of becoming a teacher at Diamondvale one day.

Unfortunately, at a young age, Voice's son got incredibly sick. He contracted an extremely rare disease that no doctor could find a cure for. Voice had never felt so powerless his entire life as he could only watch as his son's life slowly faded away.

Even years after his son's departure, Voice could not get him out of his mind. He was determined to find a way to bring back his son and that was what led to his discovery of the Geode-stones. Through years of research, he found methods of using the crystals as catalysts to make his goal a reality.

The Geode-stones by themselves would not be enough. He was required to gather additional specimens to experiment on: monkeys, gorillas, lions, and lizards were just a few.

Over time, the experiments require more time and resources from him. He needed an assistant that could efficiently run the lab without him having to be there. In time, he found a scientist capable of handling his demands, Vihaan.

Volice was so hellbent on finding a way to bring his son back that it was becoming an irrational obsession. He was convinced there had to be a solution and there came a point where he was so desperate, he was willing to trade the scientist's life for that sliver of hope.

Everyone turned to Vihaan and he confirmed everything the headmaster told them. From there, Vihaan continued the story as he noticed Volice was growing weary.

Continuing from where Volice left off, Vihaan was about to be used in an experiment but Rice appeared and saved him by volunteering to take his place.

Everyone was shocked as to why Rice would do such a thing so they allowed Vihaan to continue with the story.

Vihaan explained the complication and risk of the experiment but without hesitation, Rice accepted and was willing to go through with the process. He was able to power through the whole experiment but regardless, it failed. Volice's son could not be revived.

It was at that moment, that Volice began to realize the futility of his goal. Seeing his greatest adversary and former friend risk his life for an experiment that couldn't come to fruition opened his eyes. Volice felt defeated but Rice slowly approached him despite the discomfort on his body. He had no intention of harming Volice but had a favour to ask of him.

"What could you possibly need from me?"

"I want you to fight the students at full strength."

"You can't be serious. They will not survive..."

"I am and they will. In fact, I'm so confident about it that I will stall them on your behalf. That way, you will have absolutely no alibi when they beat you."

"Heh, you are something else. Fine, you have my word, I won't hold back against them."

Rice walked out of the lab and Vihaan followed closely behind. The instant they were out of Volice's sight, Rice collapsed on one knee. Vihaan immediately checked his vitals and he was shocked to find out how far his strength had deteriorated. His heart rate and breathing were abnormally low as he struggled to stay conscious. Vihaan knew he needed to find him medical attention immediately.

"You need to stay here and rest. Promise me you won't fight anyone."

"I don't make promises I can't keep. If you don't want me to fight, then you better hurry."

Vihaan couldn't believe his answer. He rushed towards the wilds in hopes of finding help.

Those were all the unaccounted-for events that happened. Now Volice's life force was near its end and he had some words to speak.

"If my son were still alive today, he would be the same age as all of you. Do you think you could have all been friends with him?"

Myla looked around at everyone and despite all their scars and bruises, they smiled at her. She turned back to Volice, "Yes, we would have most definitely been friends."

Her answer left a smile on the elderly man's face. "Hah, he was right, your class is something special."

His spirit faded away and the Geode-stones that were in his possession all turned to dust. Volice had finally been defeated and all the memories of the entire class returned.

Back to School

It was a new day in Diamondvale. During recess, a group of students were found on the field. Devan threw a crystal ball into the air and leaping to make an improbable catch was Sarmaan, who was now a human again.

After making the catch, he threw the ball down emphatically and began doing a weird dance with Devan. Sahil and Saivik were not too happy that they were scored on and immediately dog piled on the two. A scrap ensued with Vihaan rushing in, hoping to keep the peace.

"Hey come on guys, why can't we all just..."

"Stay out of this!" They all shouted at him.

"Sigh, here we go again..." Vihaan said in defeat.

Elsewhere on the campus, Max, Dylan, Jacob and Willyham were sharing their comic books and drawings with each other.

Jacob and Willyham were talking about their favourite comics. Willyham enjoyed the one with a regular looking hero who could beat his enemies in one hit. Then there was Jacob who had a fascination with a comic that included animatronics. They were having a great conversation until Jacob saw his little brother getting into a scrap.

"Jaden, what are you doing!?" He panicked and lefted Willyham all by himself.

Meanwhile, Max had taken one of Dylan's comics and he held it up high against the much shorter Dylan.

"Max, give it back!"

"What are you going to do about it?"

Suddenly Dylan started crying like a fountain. Willyham could hear his cry and immediately rushed to his aide.

"Max, what did you do to poor Dylan?" Willyham interrogated.

"Nothing."

"You're lying!" Accused Willyham.

"What?! I didn't do anything!"

"It appears Max might be lying. You shall be punished!"

Willyham began going crazy and chased Max around the campus.

"Dylan! I will get you for this!" Max yelled as he was running from Willyham, while Dylan was laughing."

Then there were Keira, Leo, and Sissi nearby. They each had a canvas and decided they were going to paint a picture of their school. Leo was all set and ready to paint, until he realized he didn't have any colours. He noticed Sissi was painting with all her colours so he decided to take some of hers.

"Hey! Those are my paint colours!"

"Please Sissi, I will give them back!"

"As if! You always lose things!"

"That's not true, I just haven't found them yet..."

Sissi gave him an unamused look.

"Ok fine, but can you at least tell me why you let Keira borrow them?"

"Wait what?" Sissi turned around and saw Keira subtly using her paint. "WHY DOES EVERYONE JUST TAKE MY THINGS WITHOUT PERMISSION?!" She was suddenly fuming with anger.

"I'm sorry Sissi! I won't do it again!" Keira begged for mercy.

"Now you've done it. No time to apologize, RUN!" Leo called out.

They were both scared out of their wits as Sissi chased after them with her fury.

Sitting together on a bench, Netanya and Harshitha were each reading their own book until Ashima appeared.

"I'm bored."

"You could grab a book and join us." Netanya offered.

"Can we do something a little more, exciting?"

"What?! Ashima! What could be more exciting than immersing yourself inside the world of a story?" Netanya asked with passion.

"Umm... Anything else?"

"Gasp! Ashima, let me show you what you are missing out on."

Netanya pushed up her glasses with her finger and was ready to ramble on but Harshitha couldn't stand their conversation any longer. "Sigh, how can anyone get any reading done with all the noise you two make? Ashima, what do you want to do?"

"Let's go find a teacher to disturb!"

With nothing else better to do, Harshitha followed Ashima's lead. Netanya also followed closely behind, mostly to try and persuade Ashima about the immersion of reading.

The rest could be found on the grassy field that had nets on opposing ends. They were split into two teams; Myla and Dante on one team, Ajay and Aria on the other. Arnav was the goal keeper for both teams as they only used up half the field to play.

Ajay had control of the crystal ball at his feet and he could see Dante rushing in to check him. He made a deke to the left and passed the ball to the open field. Myla thought she had an easy interception until she saw Aria running full speed ready to kick the ball.

Myla sensed her life could be in danger if she pursued the ball, so she stopped and got out of the way. Aria kicked the ball at the perfect time with all her strength and the ball flew towards the net at a blistering speed. Nevertheless, Arnav wasn't afraid, he jumped up to the left side and got just enough of the ball to deflect it off the post.

Everyone was stunned by the save Arnav had made but the play wasn't over. The ball ricocheted off the post and went directly towards an innocent bystander who was walking by. The ball hit the student right in the face and he was knocked out cold.

They paused their game and rushed over to see if the man was okay. Barmaan was lying on the ground, conscious but in a daze. Ajay, Myla, and Dante looked to Aria who kicked the ball.

"What?! Its not my fault Arnav is such a good goalie!" Arnav thanked her for the compliment, but the problem still remained. They had an injured student who needed medical attention.

From a distance, Dante's scanners were picking up an abnormally high levels of dust in the area. He looked up and saw a massive dust trail heading their way. Appearing before them with all the dust behind her, was the speedy Amrita.

"Have no fear everyone, I will take care of everything from here!"

With the help of Ajay and Dante, they got Barmaan onto a wheeled stretcher and Amrita blitzed her way to find Barmaan a real doctor as she left everyone in her dust. As they were about to return to their game, the bell sounded, alerting everyone that it was time to return to class.

It took awhile but they managed to get settled down into their seats. Entering into the room was Professor Sam who had an announcement to make. She told them that they were going to have a new self-defense teacher.

They all had mixed feelings as chatter scattered amongst them. However, the noise died down when they heard footsteps near the door. Before the door opened, a rush of memories of their former teacher returned. Then the door opened revealing their new teacher.

Student Artwork!

By: Aria

By: Dante

By: Keira

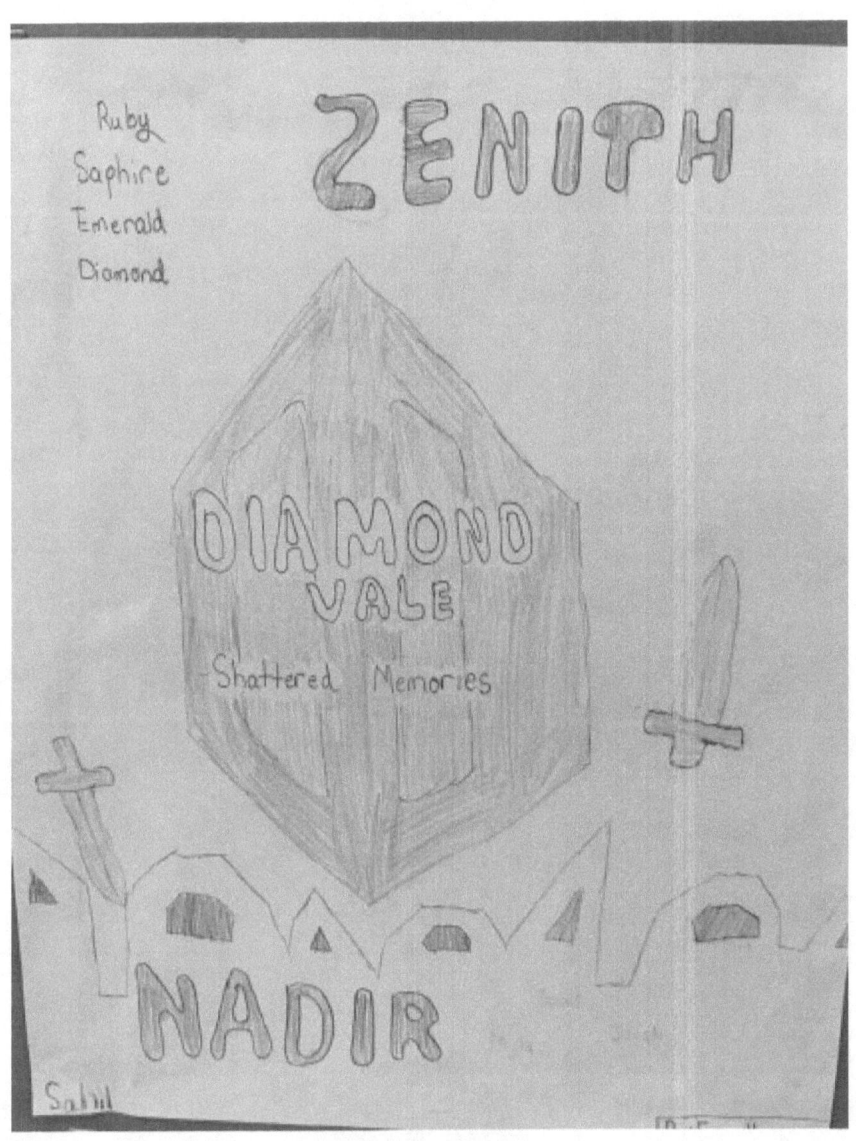

By: Sahil

By: Ajay

By: Armaan

By: William

By: Amrita

By: Dylan

By: Harshitha

By: Netanya

About the Author

Eric is a teacher out in Surrey, British Columbia. He enjoys writing books that include his students as characters in the stories. He also enjoys playing basketball and exercising.